The SCARLET BADGE

The
SCARLET

Distributed by
HOLT, RINEHART AND WINSTON, INC.
New York

BADGE

By Wilma Pitchford Hays

ILLUSTRATED BY PETER BURCHARD

COLONIAL WILLIAMSBURG
Williamsburg, Virginia

To

Grace Ann and Elliott

It was a very great race and faced peril without shrinking, down to the very boys and girls; and what the long years of the future will remember is this heroic phase, not the treaties and protocols of American History.

Cooke: *Virginia, A History of the People*

Contents

1

A Strange Party

Rob Roberts leaned forward on his horse and let the reins loose. Midnight raced across the pasture. The wind and her long black mane whipped Rob's cheeks and he laughed aloud.

At the edge of the woods he stopped Midnight. She shook her head as if she wanted to run in and out among the trees as she and Rob used to do before the revolution began. Rob pulled firmly on the right rein and turned her. The woods seemed peaceful but rebel militia might be hiding there, or raiders, or even loyalists who might not know that Rob's father was a loyalist, too.

Rob glanced toward the mansion-house of his family's Virginia plantation and hoped that his father would reach home safely before evening. Captain Roberts had been determined that Anne should have a party for her sixteenth birthday even if there was a war going on. He had promised her, too, that he would take leave of the ship he commanded for Lord Dunmore and come home, somehow, for her party.

Rob frowned. He didn't want his older sister to be disappointed, yet he couldn't feel easy until he knew his father had escaped the vigilance of the patriot committees of safety which tried to blockade every road from Norfolk where Lord Dunmore's fleet commanded the harbor and the town.

Rob pulled Midnight to a stop and looked at the sky. There was no sign of one of the thunderstorms his mother feared. The weather was warm for the eighth of December and the roads were dry. Friends from neighboring plantations could drive to the party tonight without chance of their carriages being stuck in mud.

Midnight tossed her head and tried to run again.

"Only once more to the woods and back," Rob told her.

Dinner was always at three. His mother wouldn't want him to be late when the servants had so much to do to get ready for Anne's party.

Rob sniffed the damp earth kicked up by Midnight's hoofs and the odor of pines. Deep in the woods were creeks running into the Elizabeth River which flowed to meet the waters of the James River, then on to Chesapeake Bay. Near the mouth of the Elizabeth River the towns of Portsmouth and Norfolk squatted on opposite shores like two great watchdogs.

Even in winter, the country seemed beautiful to Rob. Something kindled in him, love and pride for the land that was his by inheritance. Back, back for more than a hundred and fifty years his forebears had owned this plantation in Princess Anne County. He wanted no other life than to live here in peace with his family and friends, the way he had always lived until the rebellion began.

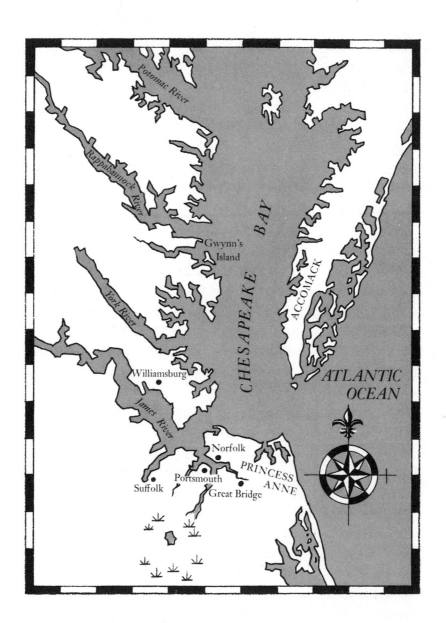

Midnight stopped short at the edge of the pines, pricked up her ears and nickered as if, this time, she sensed that the woods were dark and forbidding. Rob turned her and rode back to the stable.

He gave Midnight a quick currying and filled her feedbox with grain. Then he ran along the path through the orchard to the schoolhouse. His room was on the second floor, above the classroom, across the hall from the room of his tutor, Philip Moore.

He heard no sound from his teacher's room and knew that Philip Moore must already have gone to the big house for dinner. Hurriedly Rob washed at the basin, combed his fair hair, and changed into a clean shirt and breeches.

He ran along the oyster-shell path that bordered the garden, past the offices of the estate: the smokehouse, the dairy, the kitchen house where Lulu cooked. Juba was coming from the kitchen carrying a great tray of steaming food to the big house.

"Better hurry, Mr. Rob," Juba called. "Your papa's home and everybody sitting at the table—'cept you."

Rob took the steps of the garden porch two at a time, entered the hall, and paused outside the dining room door to catch his breath. He didn't want his father to see his relief or know that he had been worried about him.

His cousin, Becky, looked up from the table and smiled. Becky Roberts was twelve, six months younger than Rob. She had lived here since Lord Dunmore stationed his fleet before her home at Norfolk. Becky's mother was dead and her father thought she was safer on the plantation with his brother's family than she was in the town.

Becky called, "We don't have to go to school this afternoon. Mr. Moore said so."

Usually they returned to their classrooms after dinner, until five o'clock, but everything was to be different on the day of Anne's party.

Rob sat down at the table. His three-year-old sister, Sally, was on her father's lap, her head bent to listen to the ticking of his watch. Her hair was scarcely more golden than his. All the family were fair except his mother. She wore her black hair, unpowdered, high on her head in a way that made her very pretty, Rob thought. Everyone around the table, even Philip Moore, had the clear, very blue eyes of the English.

And now his father wore a uniform showing he was loyal to the English, too. Rob hadn't become accustomed to the uniform or his father's title, Captain Charles Roberts. He wished his father were wearing his worn hunting jacket and they could ride their horses over the plantation together, as they used to do.

"Papa, can you stay all night?" he asked.

"I hope so," Captain Roberts said. "Anyway, the party will last most of the night."

Rob finished dancing with Becky and followed her to the refreshment table. For the third time since the party began, he filled her plate with the foods his cousin liked best, red slices of baked ham, white slivers of roast chicken, peach tarts, and little rum cakes. When she was seated near the fire with the older women who were watching the dance, Rob went to fetch her a glass of lemon punch.

Usually he could run Becky a close race in eating, but to-

night he wasn't hungry. Although the three Negro musicians fiddled gaily, this was a strange party. On the surface people seemed to be having a good time. They were talking and laughing. Captain Roberts was smiling at Anne who sat down at the fortepiano to play for their guests.

As Rob dipped a ladle into the silver punch bowl, he thought Anne looked very pretty in her blue silk dress with its wide skirt. His father had managed to bring the dress to her although no silks or goods of any kind could be bought from England now. His mother wore a new yellow gown, and Becky preened in an ivory dress with sprigs of pink flowers.

Rob carried the full glass carefully through the groups of people to his cousin. Becky drank thirstily, then looked at him.

"Do you think Philip Moore is in love with Anne?" she asked.

Rob looked quickly at his tutor who had come a year ago from Yale College and had become almost one of the family. Philip Moore was standing beside Anne to turn the music for her. It was plain to see that they liked each other.

Rob frowned. He and his teacher were together much of the time and had become close friends, but he was troubled by some of the things that Philip Moore had said recently in the classroom. He felt sure that the young man sympathized with those rebels who called themselves patriots. Rob knew his father wouldn't like that.

"What will Uncle Charles say—about Anne and Philip Moore, if they are in love, I mean?" Becky asked.

Rob frowned again. He was troubled and mixed up about

the war. Here in Princess Anne and Norfolk Counties, many of the plantation owners and merchants of the town had remained loyal to England when the rebels drove Lord Dunmore from the Governor's Palace at Williamsburg to live on a warship in Norfolk harbor. Rob's own family were among these loyalists.

But many of their other neighbors favored the new patriot government in Williamsburg. These rebel neighbors, who were once old friends of the Roberts family, no longer came to the house or stopped to visit in front of the church on Sundays.

Rob remembered the last time his father was home and went to church. Rob had stopped with his father to speak to an old neighbor. The man had stared at the red bow on his father's breast and said, "I'd rather have seen you dead, Charles, than wearing this British badge of red."

Rob couldn't have felt worse if his old neighbor had struck him.

Now Rob looked at the red bow of cloth on his father's coat. Every man in this room wore a red bow, a scarlet badge of loyalty to England—every man except Philip Moore who wasn't a Virginian, but came from New Haven Town in Connecticut.

That's why Anne's party seems so strange, Rob thought. Only loyalists have come. Our rebel neighbors have stayed away as if we had hung out a sign of SMALLPOX.

A queer hollow feeling grew in Rob's stomach. He didn't like being shunned just because his father believed that war against the mother country was wrong.

"I wish my papa could have come tonight," Becky said, "and I miss our cousins and aunts from Williamsburg."

Rob hadn't answered her before. Becky didn't really need answers. She always had plenty more to say. But this time she sounded lonesome, so much the way Rob felt that he was disturbed and answered her impatiently.

"You know no one could come through Norfolk without a pass from the rebel Committee of Safety. If anyone traveled near Norfolk without a pass, and was caught, he'd be put in gaol."

Becky nodded and Rob was ashamed of his sharp answer.

Becky didn't need to be reminded of the danger at Norfolk. She had lived through the early troubles between the loyalists and the rebels of the town. She had seen a rebel mob drag an old shoemaker from his shop when he shouted, "God save our King and England!" The mob had stripped the old man of his clothes, dipped him by the heels in a barrel of tar, then ripped open his own featherbed and rolled him in the feathers.

Still the shoemaker sputtered, spitting feathers, "God save our King!"

The mob chased him down the street. He looked so much like a great half-plucked chicken fleeing from an axe, that Becky had covered her eyes.

She had seen loyalists on the dock at Norfolk ready to be taken on ships bound for England, leaving behind their homes and all that they could not carry with them. It was then that her father had sent her here to his brother's plantation.

"Uncle Charles said that Papa couldn't come tonight because he's on guard with the troops at Great Bridge," Becky said. "Do you think that the rebel militia is really going to attack Norfolk?"

Rob didn't answer. Almost no news reached them any more since the roads and rivers were blockaded. Yet everyone knew that Colonel William Woodford with the Second Virginia Regiment had come from Williamsburg, hoping to take Norfolk and drive Governor Dunmore's fleet of ships from the harbor. Several times in the last week, Rob had heard the distant crack of rifle fire as if rebels and loyalists had met at Lord Dunmore's fort at Great Bridge.

Rob looked at his father who was smiling and applauding with the guests when Anne stopped playing the fortepiano. He hoped the rumors of an all-out attack were not true and his father could stay at home a few days.

As the applause died, Rob heard a noise which seemed to come from the west. It sounded like the crack of thunder. He glanced quickly at his mother and saw her hand go to her throat. She was terrified of thunderstorms.

Rob couldn't understand it. She could ride the most spirited horse in the stables. She had ordered Regan, the surly overseer, to return bales of tobacco he had stolen while her husband was away. She had crossed the fields on the blackest night to tend a slave taken suddenly sick in his cabin. But whenever thunder rolled and lightning ripped the skies, his mother hurried to her bedchamber, drew the bedside curtains close and lay in the middle of her featherbed until the storm had passed.

The sound came again. The men stopped talking and listened, then moved silently to the front door and onto the lawn.

Rob saw his mother standing in the center of the ballroom floor looking anxiously after his father. Her face was so white that Rob went to her. "I'll help you upstairs, Mama," he said.

She put her hand on his shoulder. "There's no place to hide —from this storm," she said.

Then Rob knew what the sound was. It was a quick exchange of rifle shots not far from his home.

Rob ran to the doorway and heard his father say, "The firing was between us and the post at Great Bridge. Maybe it's only rebel and loyalist patrols meeting—yet it may be the beginning of Dunmore's attack."

The men pushed back into the house, called for their servants, and hurried their families into carriages. Becky ran upstairs to her room as if she did not want anyone to see that she was afraid for her father.

Captain Roberts and his wife stood at the door to tell everyone goodnight. They waved as the carriages filed under moonlight through the lane to the road. Then they looked at each other.

"Must you go to the ship tonight?" Rob heard his mother ask.

"At once," Captain Roberts answered. "If Great Bridge falls, the rebels will be in Norfolk."

"I promised Sally you'd be here in the morning when she woke," Mrs. Roberts said. "She wanted to watch the party— but I got her to bed by promising—"

"I'll go kiss the duck now," he said. He often called Sally "the duck" because her yellow hair was soft as down.

They passed Rob as if they did not see him and began to climb the wide stairs. Halfway up, on the curved landing,

Captain Roberts stooped and laughed and lifted little Sally from the floor. She was in her long white nightgown, fast asleep. He put her over his shoulder and carried her to bed.

Rob smiled. How long had his little sister watched the party from the landing before she fell asleep? She was so short, no one had seen her peeping over the bannister. Her old nurse, Mima, must have known she was there, but Mima wouldn't make the baby leave the fun. Everyone spoiled Sally.

We can't help it, Rob thought as he went outdoors. The firing had stopped. Were the rebels turning back or coming nearer?

Rob passed the kitchen, the dairy, and the smokehouse, then entered the schoolhouse and went up to his room. There was no light from under the door of Philip Moore's room across the hall. He heard voices and went to his window and looked down on the frosty moonlit garden.

Anne and Philip Moore were talking together but this time they didn't look at if they liked each other.

"Join the rebels then," Anne cried, "but if you do, never come back here."

"Anne," Philip Moore said, following her as she hurried toward the house. "Try to understand."

"I understand," Anne cried, turning to face him. "You think more of being a rebel than you do of me."

"What I feel for you—has nothing to do with my being a patriot," the young man pleaded.

Rob couldn't help feeling a little sorry for him because a girl couldn't see the logic of that.

"You taught us, right in this schoolroom," she said, "to be

loyal to our English government and law. Why don't you practice what you preach!"

She began to cry and ran down the path and into the big house. After awhile Rob heard Philip Moore climb the stairs and enter his room.

Rob was seven years younger than his teacher, but they had been close companions for a year. They had fished together and had swum in the river. They had ridden horses and gone to parties and dinners together. Rob wasn't afraid to go and talk to him now. He went across the hall and knocked at the door.

"Come in," Philip Moore said.

He was warming his hands over the last coals in the fireplace when Rob opened the door.

"I heard," Rob said, "and I have to know. Why are you taking the side of the rebels?"

Philip looked so troubled that Rob almost forgave him.

"Is it because you're from New England—that you're a rebel?" he asked.

Philip Moore looked surprised. "If you think that—I haven't taught you very well," he said. "Don't you know that many of the most influential patriots are right here in Virginia? The fighting started at Lexington and Boston—but within days a Virginia volunteer militia began marching to help them. They've been in the battles since then.

"And most of the learned men who stirred up the people and wrote the demands upon England—so the patriots could know what they're fighting for—are Virginians. You must remember that Patrick Henry with his 'Give me liberty or give me death' is a Virginian?"

"Yes," Rob said.

"Even the commander-in-chief of all the colonial armies lives here in Virginia," Philip Moore added.

Rob knew about George Washington all right. Once when he had sailed up the Potomac River with his father, he had seen Washington's beautiful plantation home overlooking the water.

"I don't understand how a gentleman like George Washington could turn rebel," he said.

"Not rebel," his teacher said. "We're patriots—doing everything we can for the good of our county—which means we have to be free of English rule."

"My father is against what England *did*," Rob said. "Papa says England needs a lesson in how to govern the colonies, but he thinks the trouble should be settled by gentlemen's agreement—Englishmen and Americans talking and reasoning together. Papa says we didn't have to fight."

"I hoped for a peaceful settlement at first," Philip Moore said, "but after the war began, I had to make a choice."

"You chose rebel," Rob said, "but I choose to be loyal to my King and the British Constitution. Papa says that we are all British subjects by law, and no other country has ever treated its subjects with more justice than England has, or offered greater freedom to its people."

Philip Moore dropped his head and looked at the fire. When he turned again, his voice showed that he was deeply moved.

"I've grown very fond of you, Rob," he said, "almost as if you were my younger brother. One of the things I like best is the way you stand up for what you believe."

He walked across the room and back. "The worst part of

this revolution is that it sets brother against brother, and friend against friend. It's a civil war really. I don't mind so much fighting the British regulars, but I don't like fighting other Americans like your father—or you—or Anne."

Rob stared at him, shaken by the mixture of anger and affection he felt for this friend.

"Yet I have to do what I believe, too," Philip said. "In the morning, I'll leave for Williamsburg to join the militia—as soon as I've told your mother that I'm going."

Rob returned to his room and sat on the edge of the bed. He was so troubled that he took off both shoes, then forgot that he was undressing, and put his shoes on again. He could scarcely believe that his good friend and teacher was leaving to join the rebels. Rob tried to think of Philip Moore as an enemy. He should feel angry and want to hurt him, but he didn't.

It's easy to know a man is your enemy if he shoots at you, Rob thought. But it's hard to hate an old friend who disagrees seriously with you for the first time.

Rob lay down on his bed. He was so tired he could think only of one thing, over and over. His sister's party had turned out to be a strange party, haunted by the disapproval of all their rebel neighbors who had refused to come. His father and mother had tried so hard to make Anne happy, but there was nothing they could do about Philip Moore's turning rebel.

A strange party and a strange unnatural war. Neighbor against neighbor. Friend against friend. Friend turned to enemy. That's what a revolution was.

2

Juba

The next morning at breakfast, Rob asked his mother, "Has Philip Moore gone?"

"Yes," Mrs. Roberts said. "Anne's upstairs crying."

One of the things Rob liked about his mother was that she didn't pretend when a question was important. Like most women she could talk pretty nonsense at a party where it was expected, but she knew when to give a direct answer.

"I heard the cannon this morning," he said. "If the rebels win, do you think they'll come this way—or march north to Norfolk?"

"I've too much on my mind to guess what the rebels'll do," Mrs. Roberts said. "Sally's in bed with a feverish cold—and the overseer has disappeared. Juba says he took everything from his cabin so he doesn't mean to come back."

"Regan was surly and a thief," Rob said, pouring honey on the hotcakes the cook, Lulu, brought him. "He's probably joined the rebels."

"I don't know who's going to keep the fieldhands working," Mrs. Roberts said. "With the war and the shortage of men I can't hire another overseer. The only servants I'm sure I can trust are Mima and Lulu, and of course, Juba."

Rob ate without really tasting Lulu's hotcakes. Mima had been his mother's nurse when she was a child, and had come here with her when she married his father. Mima was about as old as a person could be. But Juba was strong and smart. Rob knew that his father trusted Juba.

"Juba can see that the tobacco is planted," Rob said, "and we can sell it. I know the captains of the ships who take tobacco to England. I've been to the ships many times with Papa."

His mother smiled and said she'd see. "Juba has about all he can do as it is," she said.

Juba not only helped Lulu and served the family dinners, he also ran the errands. Nearly everything they needed was grown or made on the plantation, but Juba rode to Princess Anne and brought back medicinal barks and herbs from the apothecary, and the weekly newspaper, the *Virginia Gazette*, published in Williamsburg.

Since Captain Roberts had been away, Juba had to make other frequent trips. He often rode his mule to a meeting place on a certain creek below Norfolk. He carried clean clothing and letters to the Captain and brought back Captain Roberts' messages to his family.

"Your father was in such a hurry last night," Mrs. Roberts told Rob, "that he left behind an important packet of papers and his watch. I've asked Juba to take them to the meeting place today—and find out what happened at Great Bridge, if he can."

Rob and Mrs. Roberts left the table and went onto the garden porch. Juba was waiting beside the kitchen house, holding the halter of his gray mule. Mrs. Roberts gave him a packet of papers sealed with a blob of red wax and a folded letter, closed in the same way.

"His watch is inside this packet of papers," she said. "I want to be sure the Captain gets my letter so he'll know that the overseer sneaked away. Maybe you'd better ride one of our best horses this time, Juba."

Juba shook his head and climbed astride his mule. "I'd never get there on a hoss," he said. "Rebels is always looking to steal

a hoss. But no rebels seem to want to ride a mule to war. Nobody going to bother a black man on an old mule."

Mrs. Roberts smiled. "Maybe you're right," she said. "Juba, be careful. Don't wait there for him if you see or hear anyone about."

"Don't worry, Mis Roberts," he said. "I ain't never going to betray Capt'n. And don't fret about losing that overseer. He no good—that man. Me and Mr. Rob, here, we take care of everything—you'll see."

He grinned and rode away, a wiry little man who seemed to Rob much bigger than he was.

It wasn't more than ten miles to the inlet where Captain Roberts brought his ship at night when he wanted to leave or pick up a message. At high tide he could sail his sloop, *Beaver*, between the flat swampy banks of the river to the mouth of a creek lined on both sides by woods. Then he rowed a skiff up the creek a short distance to a certain dead sycamore tree, struck by lightning long ago. He sometimes met Juba there, or Juba left messages and small packages in the hollow trunk of the tree and collected any letter left by Captain Roberts.

Until now, Rob hadn't thought much about the risk his father took on these night journeys. It was true that bands of rebel militia might be encountered anywhere along the river or in the woods. But the danger was slight while the post at Great Bridge was held by Lord Dunmore's troops.

Today was different. When darkness came and Juba had not returned, Rob was worried. The fighting this morning had been in the direction of the river. Who held Great Bridge now? Where were the rebel troops?

He knew the rebels would like to capture Captain Charles Roberts. The gaol at Williamsburg was full of loyalists accused of fighting for the British. He didn't want his father in gaol. His father loved America. He just didn't hate England as the rebels did.

It was a week before Rob heard the mule's heehaw and ran to meet Juba riding up the path. Mrs. Roberts came onto the garden porch holding Sally who was still fretful with a cold.

"Is he—all right?" she asked Juba.

Juba shook his head. "I don't know, Mis Roberts, I couldn't go near that old sycamore tree. Rebel soldiers is swarming over the country like bees. A hive of 'em camped right by that dead tree the whole day whilst I hid and waited."

Anne came to the door. "Did you see any of the militia?" she asked. "Anyone—we know—I mean?"

Rob saw that Juba knew she was asking about Philip Moore.

"No, Miss Anne," Juba said, "I didn't see him."

"Did you bring back Papa's watch and the letter Mama sent?" Rob asked.

"Your mama said Capt'n got to have that packet and her letter," Juba said, "so come dark, I go on to Norfolk."

"Norfolk?" Rob cried. "You went right into the town?"

"Yes sir," Juba said. "I told you nobody going to bother a black man on an old mule."

He looked at Mrs. Roberts. "I hate to tell you, but Norfolk's full of rebel soldiers, too. They's got the whole town under their thumb.

"Gov'nor Dunmore try to drive them away. His warships fire on the town every day, but the rebels act like they's there to stay."

Mrs. Roberts bit her lower lip. Rob felt his cheeks burn. There had always been rebels in Norfolk, but the town had been controlled by Dunmore's fleet until now. He wondered what had happened to Becky's home and to their friends there.

"Did the rebels take Great Bridge, then?" Rob asked.

"They did," Juba said, "and they marched right on into Norfolk."

"Did you hear anything about the Captain?" Mrs. Roberts asked.

"No, Mis Roberts," Juba answered. "I tried. I stay right on

that dock day and night. I make myself useful, join in with men carrying pails of water to put out fires—so nobody send me away.

"Then yesteday, I see a small boat come in from the Gov'-nor's warship. That little boat come in under a white flag—brought someone real important—you could tell—he wearing one of them red coats with lots a gold braid.

"I waited and watched until that red coat and gold braid come back to the little boat and start to the warship. Then I just step up and hand him your letter and packet, and say, 'For Captain Charles Roberts, commanding the sloop, *Beaver*, sir. Thank yo kindly sir.' Then I come along home."

"You mean the British officer took the packet and letter to Papa," exclaimed Rob. "No one arrested you—or anything?"

Juba grinned. "I's here, ain't I?"

Rob couldn't tell whether his mother was laughing or crying.

"Thank you, Juba," she said. "Rob was right. We can trust you to help us manage until Captain Roberts comes home."

3

The Raid

Every day Rob hoped his father would come home or find a way to send a message, but Christmas morning arrived and no word had come from him or from Becky's father.

Rob had always loved the winter holidays which began at Christmas and lasted through Twelfth Night. Then relatives and friends came to visit for the afternoon or overnight or for several days. Rob was allowed to ride his horse on a round of visits, too.

He was related to half the families on the surrounding plantations and he had been welcome in many homes. Every table groaned with roasts of beef and pork, with goose and turkey and ham. With oyster pies and mince pies. With raisins and nuts. There was laughter, games and dancing, minuets, reels, and country dances.

This year everything was different. Many of the neighbors were no longer friends. Those who had turned rebel did not welcome loyalists in their homes or visit them. Even those who remained loyal to England, as his father had, were away fighting or afraid to leave their homes. The roads beside the woods were no longer safe.

Each night bands of men raided plantations, stealing horses, driving off cows and pigs. His mother thought that the thieves were not loyal to either side, England or the rebels, but stole to sell to the armies.

Rob knew that he would have to try hard to help his mother make this Christmas a pleasant day, as she seemed determined to do. Mrs. Roberts, Anne, and Becky, even little Sally, wore their best silk gowns. Lulu cooked a big dinner. Juba served it at a table set with the best china and silver. Rob sat at the head of the table and tried to think of interesting things to say as his father always had.

After dinner he went into the library and searched the long shelves of books for something to read to Sally. He was not good at making up stories as his father could for the little girl.

Sally curled in Rob's lap before the fireplace, but he hadn't read a page before she pushed the book away. "I don't like that story," she said and ran to her mother. "I want Papa."

Rob swallowed. Only Sally was young enough to voice what they all wanted.

Mrs. Roberts turned from the game of checks she and the girls were playing with peach stones. She lifted Sally on her lap.

"Papa will come home as soon as he can," she said.

"When?" Sally insisted. "Does he like to stay at war?"

"No," her mother said.

Anne stood up and hurried from the room.

"When Papa comes, what will he bring me?" Sally asked.

"What would you like?" Mrs. Roberts said.

"A kitten," Sally answered promptly. "I want a baby cat to sleep on my bed and play with me."

Becky looked at Rob and giggled. "She doesn't give up easily," she said.

Last week Sally had found one of the cats at the dairy with kittens so young they didn't have their eyes open. Sally insisted on taking one to the house with her. Rob had finally convinced her that the kitten was too young to leave its mother.

Now he remembered that, this morning, he had seen another cat in the stable tumbling her half-grown kittens in the hay below Midnight's feedbox.

"Sally," Rob said, "I think I know where to get you a kitten big enough to play with you."

Cool mist had brought an early dusk. As Rob walked through the orchard, he heard singing from the cabins of the field hands beyond the horses' paddocks. For Christmas his mother had sent roasts and cider to the cabins, and the Negroes were celebrating with dances and songs.

Rob entered the half-dark stable and heard the horses munching their feeding of maize. His father's red stallion Prince reared and neighed as Rob passed his stall. The big fellow hadn't enough exercise since no one dared to ride him. Mrs. Roberts' bay mare and the girls' riding horses stared as Rob went by.

When he came to Midnight, his own black filly, she nickered and thrust her head over the manger to be petted. Rob laughed.

"You knew who was coming, didn't you?" he said.

He rubbed her velvety nose before he climbed into the manger to look at the kittens.

The eyes of the mother cat narrowed suspiciously and she curled a front leg over her four babies. The light was dim. Rob bent closer to the nest in the hay. One of the feeding kittens was spotted, two were black, and a fourth was silvery-gray. Which one should he choose?

Suddenly the silver kitten reared himself upon his hind legs and struck at Rob's nose with his soft little paw. Then he lay back his ears, fluffed his tail, and crouched playfully behind his mother.

Rob had to laugh. "I'll take you, Silver," he said.

He heard footsteps running along the aisle between the stalls and he stood up. Becky had followed him.

"Rob," she whispered. "I was looking out of the window. I'm sure I saw something move at the edge of the woods."

"Maybe it's Papa or your father, trying to get home to see us," Rob said. "I'll ride Midnight to tell them it's safe—no one's here but the family."

"No, don't go, Rob," Becky said. "We don't know—who's out there—and it's night."

"I know this country better than any rebel or thief or runaway Negro," Rob said. "No one can catch me on Midnight."

Suddenly the red stallion reared and neighed angrily. Midnight lifted her head. Her ears twitched as if she heard strange sounds.

"Sh-h-h," Rob whispered.

He and Becky tiptoed to the stable door and peered around the edge. The woods which rimmed the white rails of the horses' paddock were black and still. Then Rob saw a movement under the trees.

It was a horse with a rider. Behind him were a dozen other men on horseback. For a minute Rob couldn't speak.

"Raiders," Becky whispered. "They're after our horses and stock."

"Go to the house quick," Rob commanded. "Tell Mama to lock the doors and stay inside."

"You come, too," Becky said.

"I'm going to take Midnight out to the back door," he said. "I'll hide her some place."

"In the schoolhouse," Becky cried. "The raiders will never think to look there."

She ran and pushed the back door open. Rob slipped a halter on Midnight, opened her stall and hurried her from the stable. He heard the clop of hoofs from the raiders' horses as he led Midnight through the orchard to the schoolhouse.

She balked at the narrow door. He coaxed her over the high step, pulled her head into the room, then slipped under her belly and slapped her rump. Rob felt her muscles trembling under his hand as she entered the strange classroom. He closed the door and petted and talked to her in a low voice.

"Quiet," he said, "or they'll find you."

Rob heard a crash, the squealing of pigs, the mooing of cows, the honking of geese. Frightened as he was, he had to know what had caused such an uproar. He left Midnight in the schoolhouse and ran to the pigpens.

There was Becky. She had opened the gates of the cow-barns and chased the cows toward the woods. She was running about the pigpen with a long stick chasing the pigs into the fields. She had routed the geese from their roosts in the poultry house. An angry gander took after her, his long neck stretched, hissing.

Becky ran to Rob. He grabbed her stick and chased the gander away. When he turned to Becky, she was crying.

"That mean old gander," she said. "He ruined my lovely pink sprigged dress. Just look where he ripped it."

Rob stared. How could she think of her dress at a time like this? Yet she had been quick-thinking and brave. The raiders would have a hard time trying to catch the cows or pigs or geese to roast tonight.

Rob saw a man come from the stable toward them, a short, bulky, square-built man, walking fast. He recognized the surly, runaway overseer.

"Becky," Rob said, "it's Regan. You get to the house and stay there."

This time she listened to Rob and ran.

The overseer stopped in front of Rob. His face was covered with a black stubble of beard as if he hadn't shaved for days.

"Where's *your* horse?" he demanded.

Rob knew there was no use pretending that he didn't know what the overseer meant. Midnight was a valuable thorough-bred and Regan knew every animal on the place.

"You won't find her," he said.

There was a great commotion from the stable. The red stallion shot through the door, rearing and neighing as a rider spurred him. Prince threw the rider. Several horsemen cornered the stallion against the rails of the paddock. Prince reared and struck at them with his sharp hoofs but they whipped him, flung two ropes around his neck and strangled him to submission.

Rob choked with anger. "You wouldn't dare touch Prince if my father were here," he cried.

"He ain't here—and ain't likely to be, the way things are going in Norfolk," Regan said. "Now where's your horse?"

Rob looked at the overseer. The big man could hit him. He could do anything. He wasn't going to tell where he had hidden Midnight.

Regan turned and yelled for one of his men. "Jarvis, bring that torch." Then to Rob he said, "If you want a building left on this place—you speak up. We need every horse we can get."

Jarvis came with the torch. Rob swallowed. Surely even Regan wouldn't burn the Negroes' cabins, the stables, the beautiful mansion-house. Yet if he did, the schoolhouse would burn, too, with Midnight in it.

Rob heard a shuffling of feet in the darkness beyond the paddock. Between the rails, he saw a dozen pairs of eyes watching, but no one moved to help him. He knew there was no use calling on the frightened field hands to fight against armed raiders.

"Rob," his mother called from the garden porch. "Get the horse."

He turned and walked to the schoolhouse. Regan followed. Midnight whinnied and nuzzled Rob's hair when he opened the door, as if she were glad that he was taking her from this strange stall.

The overseer took her halter rein from Rob and led Midnight into the darkness.

Rob felt so numb he couldn't even cry. His mother was waiting for him on the garden porch.

"I'm sorry, Rob," she said, "but you have to know when to fight—and when to wait for another time."

"If I ever have another chance at those rebels!" he wept.

"We don't know they're rebels," his mother reminded him

gently. "Regan could be stealing to sell to the rebels—for the money."

"A powerful lot of hosses needed to fight a war," Juba said from the darkness of the doorway.

Rob couldn't bear to think that Midnight or any of their other horses, which were almost like part of their family, should be used to fight against them.

"Why didn't you come help me," he cried to Juba. "If someone had helped—"

"I figger to be more help *alive* than dead," Juba answered. "Going to take a powerful lot of work to keep this place going until Capt'n get home."

Rob went into the house and saw Becky in her muddy pink-sprigged dress.

"What are we going to do?" she asked, "without a single horse on the plantation?"

"At least you saved the cows and pigs and geese," he said. "We'll have food."

"Where's my kitten?" Sally asked.

Rob blinked at her. She was too young to realize the pain of his loss. It took him a moment to remember what she was talking about. Then he turned and went back to the empty stable and brought the silver kitten to his little sister.

4

Davy McClain

After breakfast Rob walked into the woods to hunt the cows. He could hear the Negroes calling the pigs as they tossed maize into the pens. The squealing of the hungry pigs coming from all sides meant that the hogs would soon be penned again. The geese had come home. Only the cows remained to be found.

The morning was cold, the first time this winter that Rob had seen frost upon the ground. In a clump of pines he came upon the hoofprints of cows. He followed them through a stretch of beech and oaks and found five cows eating clumps of grass. He circled behind them, waved his arms, and shouted to start them home.

They ran in an awkward gallop but, as soon as Rob turned to hunt for more, they stopped and began to eat again. Rob was disgusted. He had to drive them home and shut them in their pasture.

He was puffing as he returned to the woods. He had never been without a horse and he had never driven cows. With so little help on the plantation now, he'd have to learn to do many things he hadn't done before.

He walked for more than an hour without seeing or hearing another cow. They have to be here somewhere, he thought. The pines grew thicker and closer together as he made his way deeper into the woods.

Above the trees he saw smoke rising from the chimney of a hut belonging to a Quaker woman. No one knew why the old woman lived alone deep in the woods so far from any other house, yet she seemed content.

Sometimes Mrs. Roberts sent Rob on horseback with special fruits from the orchard. The Quaker woman particularly appreciated the apricots and English plums. She was like no other woman Rob had ever met. After she had opened the door wide to invite him in and had thanked him, she was silent. She never spoke unless something must be said.

Finally Rob pushed through a holly thicket and came upon a creek. The water ran wide, deep, and dark with only a skim of ice trimming the banks. He knew this was the same creek to which his father came to meet Juba—but Captain Roberts brought in his skiff miles above at the creek's mouth.

Yet, Rob thought, this creek leads to the Elizabeth River which empties into the bay. If only I had a canoe, I could paddle down the creek and river to Portsmouth. Maybe I would find the *Beaver* there—or at least hear news of my father.

He was so excited at the idea that he didn't see the barge approaching until he heard the splatter of water. Two men bent their backs to pole the flat craft. A boy stood in the center of the barge. He held a lead rope fastened to a cow which followed along the bank, protesting at every step.

Rob stared, then yelled, "Stop! That's my cow."

The startled men lifted their poles. Rob ran along the creek bank to meet them. "That's my cow," he called again.

Then his heart almost stopped. Maybe these men were last night's raiders. They looked rough enough.

There was an old man with a shock of reddish white hair, and a tall boy, about a year or two older than Rob, with the reddest hair Rob had ever seen. His hair was clubbed but escaped in a mass of top curls. Both the old man and the boy were wind- and sun-browned as if they had never been under a roof. The third man was black with strong shoulder and leg muscles.

The boy leaped ashore and caught Rob by the elbow. "I have him, Grandpa," he said.

Rob jerked away and darted into the holly thicket, but the boy caught him by the collar and hauled him back. "We'll not harm you," he said, "but we canna let you go."

"Come aboard like a good lad," the old man said to Rob. "Davy speaks true. We dinna want to harm you."

It seemed senseless to struggle. He jumped onto the barge with the boy called Davy. The men began to pole again and paddle until they came to a natural pond where the creek widened and deepened.

They brought the barge alongside a small fishing boat anchored there. Her sails were furled to the mast. Her deep hull was weathered and sturdy. On the bow was carved her name, *Oyster-Shell*.

The old man climbed a rope ladder to her deck. Davy motioned Rob to follow.

"Now," the old man said when they were standing face to face. "What's this—about the cow?"

"It's mine," Rob said. "You know it. Wasn't it enough that you stole every horse we had?"

The old man's face darkened. "Watch your tongue, lad. Who stole what?"

"Raiders stole every horse on our plantation last night," Rob said. "They'd have the cows too, if my cousin hadn't chased them into the woods."

"It never was us," Davy said. The Scotch burr in the boy's voice was much less than in his grandfather's.

"Whose plantation?" the old man asked again.

"Captain Charles Roberts, sir, with Governor Dunmore's warships in the harbor," Rob answered proudly.

"Captain Roberts?" Davy cried. "We're to meet him—"

Davy's grandfather gave him a warning look and the boy stopped.

"Please, sir," Rob asked. "Do you know where Captain Roberts is?"

The old man looked closely at Rob. "It's a very strange thing," he said, "a very strange thing indeed, for you to be bringing *that* name to this place—spying on us—calling us thieves!"

"I wasn't spying. And I'm sorry I called you raiders," Rob said. "Please tell me what you know about my father."

"If he *is* your father," the old man said.

"He is. I'm Rob. Robert Roberts. My father commands the sloop *Beaver*. We haven't heard from him since the night the rebels captured Great Bridge. The rebel soldiers are camped at the inlet where he used to meet Juba so we can't write to him or hear from him."

The old man's eyes twinkled. "You speak well, lad. More than that—you look just like him. Davy, do you think we can trust the lad?"

"Aye, Grandpa," Davy said and grinned at Rob.

"I'm David McClain," he added. "My father's fighting with the Queens Loyal Volunteers. Grandpa McClain and I do what we can to supply Lord Dunmore's fleet of ships with provisions."

"There's few enough to help—and proud we are to serve Britain." Captain McClain said. "Your father, knowing the country the way he does, helps by pointing out plantations where we can get provisions. He meets us and takes the supplies to the Governor's ships."

That's why Papa came so often to the river, Rob thought.

"About the cow, now," Captain McClain said, "We found her wandering alone—lost by rebel raiders we thought—and helped ourselves. But I doubt Captain Roberts will welcome us bringing his own animal, even to feed the Governor's soldiers. The cow will go with you home."

"Let me go with you to meet my father," Rob pleaded.

Captain McClain shook his head. "No lad, your father'd not forgive us letting you take such a risk."

"We won't go upriver until dusk, when the tide brings in high water," Davy said. "Come away down and eat with us before you go."

There was more room in the deep hull of the small ship *Oyster-Shell* than Rob expected. It was loaded with bags of grain and a half-dozen pigs ready for roasting. He knew that his cow would have been with them in a short time if he hadn't come along.

Rob and Davy squeezed onto a bench behind a small table in the cabin. Captain McClain sat across from them on a bunk.

"We can't have a fire," Davy said. "But we've oysters and fine boiled rockfish."

Rob found the cold fish delicious. There were flat cakes made of coarsely ground maize, too, with mugs of milk which the big Negro brought.

"Courtesy of your own cow," Captain McClain said raising his mug.

Rob smiled but he felt troubled. "Do you steal most of the

supplies you take to the ships?" he asked. "Does my father—?"

"No, lad," Captain McClain assured him. "Your cow was a bit of forage—but there's many a loyal planter glad to sell food for his suffering friends on the Governor's fleet of ships. We only transport it."

"When the rebels took Norfolk," Davy explained, "many loyalist families fled to the Governor's ships for protection. They have to live on the water in any ship that could be found. In sloops, schooners, warships, even old fishing boats. The rebel Committee of Safety ordered no one to sell to the Governor's ships—yet you ken they must eat."

"Then my father is breaking the law, too, when he brings food to the ships," Rob said.

"Your father's acting under orders," Captain McClain said sternly. "Remember lad, war's not bonny. Maybe your father's got no more use for Governor Lord Dunmore than I have. Dunmore's a fool who's never done a thing right since trouble began between the colonies and England. But men like your father and me—we're loyal Virginians. Good Americans. We love this country as much as any son-of-liberty. But we've pondered on what revolution means—and we think England, when she's come to her senses, can govern us better'n rebels."

Rob's heart beat faster. "Papa said that Governor Dunmore could overcome the rebels if only the English general would send some of his ships from Boston to help."

"So we could," Captain McClain said, "that's what we're waiting and hoping for."

Davy said, "You should see, Rob, how much the people on the ships need food. Warships weren't made for women and children to live on. Even sloops and schooners don't make good homes for long. Every ship is so crowded, people have to sleep in rows on the floor. It's cold, and many of them are sick with smallpox and fevers."

Rob couldn't help feeling sorry for the anxious homeless families on board the fleet of ships in the harbor before Norfolk. Yet he knew it was dangerous to be carrying food to them.

"How do you go freely back and forth?" Rob asked. "How do you get past the rebel guards along the shores of the towns?"

The old man finished his mug of milk. "Lad," he said, "we run with the fox and hunt with the hounds."

Rob thought that over. "You mean the rebels think you're rebel—and the loyalists know you're loyal?"

"Something like that," Captain McClain said. "McClains have been fishing and oystering out of Portsmouth for fifty years. We go and come any place we like over the bay and rivers tending to our own business just as we always have—neutral-like."

"And the rebels don't suspect you," Rob said. "Are you spies, too?"

"We'd pay heed to information if it came while we worked," Captain McClain said, "but our real job is to take food by night to soldiers like your father."

"And to the poor women and children living afloat," Davy added. "You must never tell, Rob. We trusted you."

Rob saw the Captain watching him. His eyes were the cold gray color of a winter's sky.

"Aye, lad," the old man said. "I think it will be a very good thing now if ye was stepping off to your home. And pay heed, never come back here. If ye was followed—and we captured— they could get your father, too."

Davy went up on deck with Rob and rowed him to shore. "The war will end—soon I hope. Then you'll be more than welcome on the *Oyster-Shell*," Davy apologized for his grandfather's order not to return.

"Please tell my father that our horses were stolen," Rob said as he led his cow away, "but tell him not to worry. We're all right."

5

The Quaker Woman's Hut

The months of winter passed without a word from Captain Roberts or his brother, Becky's father. To Rob the three months seemed longer than any year had ever been. Now and then Juba brought home a copy of the *Virginia Gazette,* and Rob read something of what was happening around him.

In February, the commander of the colonial troops had ordered the remaining buildings in Norfolk to be burned. If there was no town, he said, Dunmore wouldn't have a place to return to, and the country would be rid of the Governor and his warships.

But after the burning of Norfolk, the British sent the frigate *Roebuck* with troops to help Dunmore. The Governor moved across the channel and took possession of Portsmouth.

Yesterday's newspaper had stated that Major-General Charles Lee had arrived in Williamsburg on March 29th. He hoped to raise cavalry to attack Portsmouth and capture that town for the rebels.

While Rob worked in the vegetable garden, he thought of his father and Becky's. They must be at Portsmouth. If only he knew how they were.

He heard a scream and ran to find Becky with her back pressed against the garden porch. She was trembling. Her face was so white that the freckles across her nose stood out like spots on a turkey egg. She pointed toward the steps.

"It's only a lizard," Rob said. "It's come out to take the afternoon sun. You scared me half to death, Becky."

"It ran across my ankle," Becky said and shivered.

Sometimes Rob found it hard to remember how brave Becky had been the night of the raid. She hadn't even cried when she learned that the rebels had burned her home in Norfolk with all that she and her father owned. She only practiced longer each day at the fortepiano with Anne to show her father, when he came, that she was learning the graces a young lady must know when they had a home again.

Yet she shuddered at the touch of a little lizard. Rob shook his head.

"Come see how much my peas have grown," he said.

He had never paid much attention to the garden when there were gardners to tend it. But this spring he had planted the vegetables with his mother's help. Even Anne and Becky, wearing gloves and wide hats to protect their complexions, had learned to weed the flowerbeds and pick strawberries.

Becky admired the rows of peas, three inches high, then went to gather cowslips and violets bordering the garden.

Rob wondered what his father would think if he knew

there was no tobacco crop on the plantation this year. Rob had discovered that he and Juba knew nothing about the growing of tobacco, and field hands had to be directed. Mrs. Roberts decided that the few remaining Negroes should plant maize to feed the animals. So there were no tobacco seedlings to be transplanted.

Rob glanced beyond the stables toward the seedbeds full of weeds. He thought he saw a movement in the open door of the stable. Then a tall man appeared and hurried through the orchard. Rob couldn't move as he saw the fair hair under the tricorn hat, the smile in the blue eyes, and felt his father's hand on his shoulder.

Becky ran ahead of them to the house shouting, "Aunt Margaret, Anne, Sally! Uncle Charles is home."

When they were in the house, Rob was pushed to the edge of the circle of women hugging and kissing his father. Sally wouldn't take her arms from around her father's neck until Lulu and Juba had covered the dining table with a fine dinner and they were all seated to it.

"Tell us where you've been," Anne said. "Tell us everything."

"Where is my papa?" Becky asked.

"He wanted to come, but he's stationed on a warship," Captain Roberts said, "He sends you his love."

"I've worried," Mrs. Roberts said. "Every day I hoped for a letter from you."

"If there was time to write, I had no one to bring a letter— no one I could trust. Letters are intercepted now and broken open. The rebels want to learn about our movements and condition."

"Davy could bring a letter," Rob said.

His father looked at him and Rob's cheeks grew hot. He hoped that no one else had noticed what he said. He had kept his promise not to tell about Davy and Captain McClain.

"I'm sorry you lost Midnight," his father said. "And I wish I had one of our horses to ride back. It's a long walk to the mouth of the creek."

"Do you have to return tonight, Charles?" Mrs. Roberts asked.

"As soon as it's dark," he said. "It was a risk to come at all— the rebels are everywhere. But I had to see how you were. Has the Committee of Safety visited you? Asked any questions?"

"No," Rob said.

His father seemed relieved. "Major-General Lee wants to confiscate the property of every Tory on the blacklist and send him to prison, and remove his family from Virginia," he said.

Rob knew his father was listed as an enemy of America. Every loyalist who had taken up arms and joined Dunmore was on the list. Rob had never dreamed that this placed his home in danger.

"You mean," he asked, "that the rebel government at Williamsburg can take our house and all our land just because we don't agree with them?"

"In some places loyalists have already lost their property," his father said. "We can thank Providence that the members of the Committee of Safety here don't like to take homes from women and children."

"What about burning our homes in Norfolk?" Becky said.

"Norfolk was a battleground," Captain Roberts said.

"That's different from selling our home to the highest bidder and telling us to leave the country. Exile from the land you love is cruel punishment."

Suddenly Rob couldn't finish eating his strawberries and cream. "I never want to leave this plantation," he said. "Papa, I wouldn't know where to go if I ever had to leave Virginia."

His father looked at Rob. "I wouldn't either," he said.

They sat around the table and talked until Rob noticed that no more sunlight came through the windows. He wanted to be sure it was safe for his father to leave the house. He went onto the garden porch and looked in all directions.

In the dusk the plantation was peaceful. He could hear a banjo and singing from the Negro cabins. There wasn't a person in sight across the fields to the woods.

When Rob returned to the dining room, his mother looked as if she were trying not to cry. Everyone remembered more things to say. Captain Roberts kept stopping on his way to the garden door.

"Did you receive the packet of papers and your watch?" Mrs. Roberts asked.

"Yes, I forgot to tell you. It's been so long," he answered.

When the knock came the Captain was close enough to answer himself, but he motioned Rob to the door and the women to return to the table. Then he slipped behind the full tapestry curtains which hung to the floor on the windows beside the door.

Sally tried to follow him. Becky caught her hand. "Sh-h, don't look," she said. "We'll play he isn't home."

Rob waited until the full curtains had stopped moving. When his father was hidden, Rob opened the door. He hoped the four men standing there in rebel militia uniform couldn't hear his heart pounding.

"We're looking for Captain Roberts," one of them said. "Is he home?"

"Philip Moore," Rob stammered. "What—what are—you doing here?"

"I was ordered to come," the young man said stiffly. "I know the country well."

Anne appeared behind Rob. "You should!" she cried. "How dare you come after my father when he's been so good to you."

Rob thought his former tutor looked even more unhappy than he had the night he and Anne quarreled in the garden. "We found your father's skiff at the mouth of the creek," he said. "We have orders to capture him. We want to take him peacefully here. I don't want to have to shoot him—if he tries to run."

Anne put her hands over her face and turned into the dining room.

Mrs. Roberts came forward. "Mr. Moore," she said as if she were delighted to see him. "We've finished dinner but there's plenty left for you and your friends. You must be hungry."

The men hesitated, looked at one another, stepped into the hall. They cast longing glances through the open dining room door at the table. Rob couldn't believe his mother was going to feed these enemies who stood within inches of the heavy curtains behind which his father was hidden. She was leading the way, showing them where to sit, ignoring their rebel uniforms and guns.

"Anne," she said, "please help me keep these young men company while they eat."

"I won't," Anne said.

Mrs. Roberts came to her and said in a low voice, "Whoever sits at our table is your guest, Anne. Remember that."

Anne went and sat opposite the men. Then Rob understood. His mother had seated all four men with their backs to the garden door. Anne sat across from them to be looked at!

Rob saw Sally glance toward the curtains where his father hid and he felt sick. Becky caught the little girl's hand and said, "I hear Kitty crying for you upstairs."

Mrs. Roberts began to serve the men and asked them whether they liked dark or light meat. Rob knew this was the time for his father to escape, but the men would hear the garden door open and look around—unless—unless they thought *someone else* was leaving through that door.

"Mama," Rob said clearly, "I'll go to the dairy and get more strawberries and cream."

He opened the door. Captain Roberts slipped from behind the curtains onto the porch. Rob followed, and closed the door. They ran through the darkness to the stable.

"I hoped the rebels had left their horses here," Captain Roberts said.

"Probably tied them in the woods," Rob said.

"How I wish I had my Prince or your Midnight," his father said.

"You could ride Juba's mule," Rob suggested.

"They'd catch me on a slow mule. I can hide in the woods better on foot."

"They found your skiff," Rob said. "Where can you go?"

"Captain McClain's coming up the creek with provisions tonight," Captain Roberts said. "If I can reach him—"

"I'll show you where he anchors the *Oyster-Shell*," Rob said.

A horse whinnied from the edge of the woods. A dog barked from a Negro's cabin. The door of the big house opened. A man stood in the light, then ran down the steps of the garden porch. He was followed by the other three soldiers. They were going for their horses.

"Do you think they know you're home?" Rob asked.

"I'm afraid so," his father answered, "unless they're after you—because you didn't bring back the strawberries and cream."

Rob tried to smile at his father's attempt to joke.

"Let's go," Captain Roberts said.

They kept close to the rails of the paddock, ran across the field and into the woods. They could hear the men on horseback crisscrossing under the trees searching for them. It was dark but moving shapes could still be seen if the men came close enough.

"Bend low, keep to the shadows," Captain Roberts warned.

Rob followed his father in a dogtrot, keeping close to the holly and thickest pines. They came to a clearing and hesitated. Should they try to cross the open place or flank it? Then close behind them, they heard brush crackling as a horse and rider pushed through.

Captain Roberts drew his small gun. Rob was almost smothered by the pounding of his heart. He didn't want his father caught—but he didn't want Philip Moore shot. He swallowed the warning cry in his throat.

His father pocketed his gun and whispered, "Climb a tree, get well up among the branches."

They scarcely reached the shelter of thick pine boughs before a horse and rider passed under them. Rob felt sure he knew they were there, but the rider went on. Soon three horsemen followed.

They stopped at the edge of the clearing, then parted, one of them flanking each side and two searching the tall meadow grass.

"Wait a little longer," Captain Roberts said. "They may come back."

While they waited, the air turned cold. A flash of lightning zipped across the sky far out over Chesapeake Bay. Thunder rumbled after it. One of the frequent spring storms was on its way. Scattered drops of rain pattered on the pine needles.

Captain Roberts said, "The McClains can't go up the creek in this storm."

In a few moments the woods were roaring with wind and rain. Rob and his father jumped to the ground and ran.

"Where can we go?" Rob shouted above the deepening rolls of thunder.

"Not back home," his father said. "That's where the rebels will look again."

"The Quaker woman's hut," Rob said. "She'll take us in and it's not far from the *Oyster-Shell's* anchorage."

"Of course," his father said. "I can go on alone from there in the morning if you point the way for me."

Jabs of lightning lit the dark woods as they jogged the miles to the hut. Water ran from their clothes in streams when they knocked upon the door.

The Quaker woman came finally, her hand cupped around a candle flame. She peered at their faces and must have recognized them. She didn't say a word.

"May we stay here tonight?" Captain Roberts asked.

She moved back from the door and let them enter. They went to the fireplace where a few coals glowed feebly. They were shivering. Captain Roberts put a log on the fire.

The old woman brought them a blanket and two of her great wool petticoats. She went back to the cubicle which hid her bed.

Captain Roberts and Rob stripped off their cold dripping clothes and hung them to dry on pegs by the fireplace. They stepped into the petticoats and pulled them high under their arms.

The log had begun to blaze and give some light. Rob looked

at his tall father in the full red wool petticoat which reached only to his knees. He looked down at his own gray petticoat touching the floor around him like a tent.

Rob grinned and his father smiled. They began to laugh then until tears ran down their cheeks.

But when they had spread the blanket on the floor and had lain down before the fire Rob couldn't sleep. A lump had come in his stomach when he heard his father laugh. It was a feeling of homesickness, although he wasn't far from home.

He was homesick for the way things used to be when his father often laughed like that. When Philip Moore was his friend, not an enemy who chased him through the woods. Until a few months ago when it became a crime to be a loyalist, there had been joy in their home. Friends, neighbors, and relatives came to dinner, talked together, liked and helped each other.

That's what I miss most, Rob thought. I want the hating to stop. I want to like people and people to like me. And most of all, I want the war to end and my father to come home to stay.

6

Shipwreck

R ob and Mrs. Roberts were picking the first mess of peas. "The pods aren't filled yet," she said, "but everyone is hungry for fresh green peas."

Rob remembered that his father liked young peas in the pod. He hadn't heard from his father since the night they slept in the Quaker woman's hut, six weeks ago. But he must have reached the *Oyster-Shell* and escaped safely. The *Virginia Gazette* had not listed Captain Charles Roberts among the loyalists confined in Williamsburg gaol.

A whirl of dust traveled between two rows of peas. The sun darkened. Mrs. Roberts glanced apprehensively at the sky.

"It's gone past us," Rob assured her.

He couldn't blame his mother for being anxious. There had been more storms this spring than any year he could remember. Only last week the worst storm of the season had come suddenly from over the bay while the family was eating a late dinner.

One minute the evening sun had been shining. The next moment clouds as black as smoke rolled over the house. Each streak of lightning seemed to have two arms which reached and jabbed and trimmed black clouds in a glow of fiery red. Wind rattled the windows. His mother had excused herself from the table— something she would never have done for any ordinary reason—and hurried upstairs to draw the bedside curtains around her.

"Rob," his mother said now, "there's someone coming across the garden—a boy with curly red hair."

Rob turned, almost upsetting his basket of peas.

"It's Davy," he said. He had told his mother about the McClains so she would know how his father escaped from the rebels six weeks ago.

Mrs. Roberts stood up. Rob got to his feet and waved.

When Davy reached them he said at once, "I brought something to you." He handed Rob a gold watch and chain.

Rob held it in his palm for his mother to see. "Papa's watch," he said. "Where did you get it?"

"Captain Roberts sent it to you," Davy answered. "He said it was his father's and he wanted his son to have it."

"Please," Mrs. Roberts said. "Where is my husband?"

"I don't know," Davy said, "but—"

"Then where did you get the watch?" Mrs. Roberts cried. "Why did he send it home to Rob? Is he alive?"

"He was when I saw him," Davy said.

"Then why?" Rob asked.

"'Twould be more quickly told if I began at the beginning," Davy said.

"Then come in out of the heat," Mrs. Roberts said. "You

must be hungry. Rob, call Anne and Becky. Don't wake Sally. She's still feverish and needs her nap."

"Well," Davy said, when they were all at the table waiting for Lulu to prepare something for him to eat. "It was last week, the night of the big storm."

Everyone nodded. They were not likely to forget last week's storm.

"Grandpa and I sailed over to Accomack to help with the horses."

"Help with horses—on Accomack?" Rob interrupted.

"Aye," Davy said, "but that's another story. We went there for the horses, but the storm came. We had to pull into an inlet or the *Oyster-Shell* would have been dashed to pieces against the shore.

"Early next morning we started to leave, when we saw a white flag above the trees which covered the narrow strip of land between us and the bay. It seemed a strange place for a flag. Grandpa said it must be a call for help from one of the ships which had come to meet us last night."

"Was it?" Rob asked.

Davy continued, "We didn't know. And we didn't know what to do. While crossing the bay, we had seen a regiment of rebels camped on a point about three miles above. We hoped to get away before they discovered us, but Grandpa decided to cut across the wooded peninsula and see who was flying the white flag."

"Was it my father?" Rob asked.

"It was," Davy said. "The storm had driven and piled his ship onto the beach. It was full of cargo, and the tide was low. He couldn't get it afloat."

"What did he do?" Rob asked.

"Hush, Rob," his mother said, "let Davy tell us."

"Our men waded out," Davy went on. "We pushed and dug the sand. Captain Roberts finally ordered his crew to throw the provisions overboard to lighten the sloop, except the horses which we couldn't get out of their slings in the hold, the way the ship lay.

"It was no use. The *Beaver* was stuck, listing almost on her side in shallow water.

"Grandpa told Captain Roberts that we'd go back and bring the *Oyster-Shell* around the peninsula and take him and his men off.

"Before we reached the trees, we saw a man in civilian clothes put to sea in an old canoe and paddle out to the ship. We stopped at the edge of the woods and watched him go on board and talk to Captain Roberts.

"Then all at once the shore swarmed with rebel soldiers. I don't know how they crept up so quietly. They launched a rowboat with a gun in her and circled to the back of the *Beaver*.

"Captain Roberts called to them and said he couldn't fight. His powder was wet. His guns filled with water. His second officer was injured and he had sick men in the hold.

"After much shouting back and forth, the rebels cautiously waded out and took him and all the men. They even captured the civilian in the canoe. They let him go, finally.

"He was the Reverend McTyon—but we didn't know that until later when he circled through the woods to the *Oyster-Shell* and told us.

"He said he was the minister of the parish nearby. He had gone out to see if he could help Captain Roberts. When the Captain saw the rebels coming, he gave the Reverend Mc-Tyon his watch and asked him to give it to Grandpa and me—to bring to you, Rob."

No one said anything for a moment. Rob looked at the watch he had seen his father wear so often. He must have been in grave danger to have sent it home.

"Do you know where they took my husband?" Mrs. Roberts asked.

"The Reverend McTyon said Captain Roberts expected to be taken to the gaol in Williamsburg," Davy answered.

"He isn't listed," Rob said.

"There hasn't been time," Mrs. Roberts said. "We must know if they took him to Williamsburg!"

Rob knew his mother would feel relieved to know his father was alive even if he were found in gaol. Juba couldn't go this time. He had been sick with fever and ague for several days.

"I'd go to Williamsburg," Rob said, "but will the rebels stop me?"

"Even the rebels won't keep a boy from visiting his father in gaol," Mrs. Roberts said. "You can ride Juba's mule and cross on the ferry."

Rob wanted to see his father, but he didn't like the idea of riding an old mule down Duke of Gloucester street, where he had ridden Midnight so proudly on his last visit to his cousins.

Davy saw how unhappy Rob looked and said, "Grandpa and I could take you in the *Oyster-Shell* to Portsmouth and up the James River, then you'd have to walk five or six miles through fields and woods to Williamsburg."

"I'd rather walk twenty miles than ride that old mule into town," Rob said.

"Then get ready," Davy said.

Lulu came with Davy's dinner. Anne and Becky talked to him while Mrs. Roberts packed clean clothing for her husband.

"Take him the green peas, too," she said to Rob, "and cakes and a jar of peach preserves. I'm told the food is terrible at the gaol."

When Rob was ready with a package under each arm, he joined Davy. Mrs. Roberts with the girls followed the boys onto the garden porch.

"I don't know where you should stay," she said. "Your younger cousins usually visit in the country this time of year."

Rob knew he was related to a dozen families in the town by blood or marriage. Would they welcome him since his father was a loyalist? He remembered their hospitality in the past and somehow he couldn't believe that anyone in Williamsburg would hurt him or his father, even if many of them were rebels now.

"Go to your Aunt Lucy's," his mother decided finally. "Lucy and I are like sisters. My mother brought her up with me after her mother died. And Lucy knows everyone and everything that happens in the town—on both sides. Her husband's a rebel but her brother's a loyalist."

"What's a loyalist?" Sally asked, coming to the porch, rubbing sleep from her eyes and hugging her silver kitten.

Mrs. Roberts answered the little girl, "A loyalist is a loyal British subject—who, at the same time, loves Virginia with all his heart and is proud to be an American."

Rob was moved by her words. "Like Papa," he added.

As the boys crossed the garden and fields to the woods, Rob asked, "Why did you go to Accomack for horses? You can't carry horses in your small boat."

"The horses are loaded onto larger ships," Davy explained.

"We go over to help bring them from the horse pens to the shore. We have to work fast to get them loaded at night, and get away before daylight."

"Where do you take the horses?" Rob asked. "Aren't Governor Dunmore's men on ships?"

"They still need horses for the men on shore at headquarters," Davy said, "and we ship to loyalists fighting in the north. So many horses are killed in battle we always need more."

Rob thought of Midnight and he was troubled. Was a rebel soldier riding Midnight? Did he feed and curry her properly?

"Raiders have taken most of the horses on the plantations near us," Rob said. "How can you find so many on Accomack?"

"Wild horses," Davy said. "We held a roundup last fall on the islands."

Rob looked at him in surprise. He knew about the wild horses which had roamed for more than a hundred years through the scrub pine and marshes of Chincoteague and Assateague Islands. Sailors on passing ships often reported seeing the little wild horses plunge into the sea and swim from island to island.

"I didn't know anyone rode those little ponies," he said.

"Some of them are fine good horses," Davy said.

"Where do you keep them? Don't the rebels find so many wild horses in pens?"

Davy explained, "After the roundup last fall, loyalist farmers and planters on Accomack each took a few horses home and broke them to ride. They bring them to the shore on an appointed day—only twenty or thirty horses at a time, so they won't be missed. The rebels don't know where to watch for us. We never ship from the same place twice. That's why we need so many men—we have to make human fences of ourselves when we drive the horses to the water."

Rob was so excited that he stopped and looked at Davy. "Take me the next time," he begged. "I'm good with horses. I can help."

"I'll ask Grandpa," Davy promised. "We won't go again before you're home from Williamsburg, if you're coming back on Friday."

7

Williamsburg Gaol

D you think they'll let Papa leave the gaol on parole?" Rob asked Aunt Lucy when she showed him to the room at the head of the stairs where he would sleep.

She was dressed to go to a party. Her curled powdered wig made her seem forbiddingly tall, but her eyes were kind.

"Let us hope so," she said. With the flame from her candle she lighted another on a chest beside Rob's bed. "Although the name of Charles Roberts will bring you no friends in Williamsburg. The people are very put-out with anyone who accepted a commission from Lord Dunmore."

Rob swallowed. "Will—will they let me see Papa?" he asked.

"They have nothing to fear from a boy," she said, "and you can take one of my strawberry pies to sweeten the gaoler's temper."

The next morning Rob walked along Nicholson street carrying a strawberry pie neatly balanced on top of the two packages for his father. He had to peer around the sides to keep from running into men who hurried toward the taverns and ordinaries for breakfast.

He had not expected to see so many carriages and men on horseback on this hot humid day in May. They must be the delegates who had come from all over Virginia for the convention which was meeting in the town.

Last week after governing British Virginia for 157 years, the House of Burgesses had declared itself dissolved. The same day a new convention had been called to decide upon a form of government for the Commonwealth of Virginia. Rob thought that he had come to Williamsburg at an exciting time. He would have so much to tell when he met the McClains on Friday and returned to his home.

Rob slowed his steps as he approached the massive brick walls of the Public Gaol. He saw a poor wretch with arms and head padlocked in the pillory where everyone could see his shame. This man would not be his father. No one would treat Charles Roberts like that, Rob thought.

When he had given the pie to the gaolkeeper and was shown into the small airless room where his father was imprisoned with a dozen men, Rob thought the pillory might be better than this.

There was only one small window. The room was hot as an oven and the light dim. The odors of unwashed bodies and decay made Rob sick at his stomach. He wanted to turn and run after the gaoler, but the heavy doors clanged behind him.

Rob tried not to shudder at the sight of a groaning old man in leg irons and the smell of burning tar in an iron pot. Then he saw his father rise from the matted straw which covered the dirt floor. He caught Rob's hands.

"Rob, I'm so glad to see you," he said. "How are you? Tell me of your mother and Sally, and Anne and Becky? Are you all well?"

Rob nodded. He couldn't trust himself to speak. His father, who was always neat and clean, was wearing a torn uniform. His linens were stained as if they had not been changed since his capture.

"Mama sent clean clothes and food," he said.

Captain Roberts led him to dim light which came through the small barred window. "I want to see you," he said and

looked closely at Rob's face. "Thank your mother for me when you get home, and don't tell her how crowded we are. We're all loyalists in this cell."

Rob heard a groan.

"Poor old John Goodrich has a fever and is restless under his chain," Captain Roberts said. "A doctor came this morning. He ordered the old man to be taken from the prison. He must have fresh air—or he'll die."

Rob almost wished that his father were ill so he would be taken from this place.

"Do you think you can get out on parole?" he asked. "Aunt Lucy says that many loyalists have taken the oath not to fight against the rebels. Loyalists have to stay right on their own plantations—they can't go anywhere—and some of them paid large fines. But, Papa, you could come home and stay if you took the oath."

For a moment Captain Roberts didn't answer. He looked at Rob. "I've already been sentenced by a County Commissioner's Court," he said, "but I've appealed to the Convention. I hope—for your mother's sake and you children—that the Convention will hear me."

"They will," Rob said. "I'm sure they will. Aunt Lucy said that Mr. Ralph Wormley went before the Convention a few days ago, and declared that he was *for* the American cause. He said he only differed from public opinion in the *way* of forcing Britain to listen to American demands.

"The Convention settled his case by exiling him to his father's estate in Frederick. If they let Mr. Wormley go, they'll let you go, Papa."

"Ralph Wormley only wrote a letter which the members

of the Convention thought showed an unfriendly and dangerous spirit," Captain Roberts said. "He wrote the letter to a
friend, but it was opened by the rebels' Committee of Safety."

"But they let him go," Rob said.

"After he posted a bond of ten thousand pounds that he
would never break his exile," Captain Roberts said. "Ten
thousand pounds! If they gave a sentence like that to Ralph
Wormley for writing a critical letter—what can I expect? Be-
sides, I'm not asking for parole. I'm asking the Convention to
reverse the sentence passed upon me by the County Commissioner's Court of Accomack where I was captured."

Rob had never seen his father downhearted before and he
was distressed. "You have friends in town," he said. "Lots of
people used to come to our house for dances and picnics and
to hunt with you, Papa."

"We'll see how much my friends will do now," Captain
Roberts said. "But don't fret. I hear the gaoler coming for you.
Tomorrow bring me paper and a pen. I want to write to your
mother."

Rob scarcely saw or heard anything as he walked away
from the gaol. His father was an officer under Lord Dunmore.
He had fought against the rebels at Norfolk. He had been
captured in the act of bringing provisions to the British warships at Portsmouth. There was no use trying to pretend that
he was not in grave danger. What would they do to him?

Rob had been so shocked to find his father in such a dismal
crowded room that he hadn't even remembered to ask what
penalty the County Commissioner's Court of Accomack had

demanded. What was the sentence his father was now appealing before the Convention?

The clopping of horses' hoofs overtook Rob as he returned along Nicholson Street. Militiamen on horseback passed him. He saw a black filly and his heart leaped. She looked like Midnight. He ran along beside the horseman and called to her.

The black horse did not turn her head. Rob moved back to the sidewalk. Midnight would have known him and nickered no matter how tightly her rider held the reins.

He wished he knew where his horse was. He thought, too, of Philip Moore. Was his former friend among the militia at Williamsburg? The town was teeming with men who were on their way to join the rebels at Norfolk. Aunt Lucy said everyone believed that the rebels were almost ready to attack Dunmore at Portsmouth.

Rob came to Market Square. An unusually large group of people was gathered in front of the courthouse. He stopped behind men reading a handbill. Its message seemed to excite them.

"They've done it!" a man shouted. "The Convention has bid his Majesty goodbye forever!"

Another man cried, "I give you, Virginia! For freedom and independence!"

A third man dropped his head and walked away. His face was white. Rob could barely hear what he said, "I never believed it would come to this!"

Troubled, Rob turned and walked until he came to the

white picket fence which enclosed his aunt's garden. He saw
Aunt Lucy in her garden and went to her. She had a basket
over her arm as if she had planned to cut flowers to arrange
for the house. But she didn't seem to know what to pick. She
just stood and looked at him.

He told her about the excitement of the men on the green.
She brushed back his hair with her hand.

"I know," she said. "Yesterday the new Virginia Convention passed a resolution directing the Virginia delegates in
Congress—to propose and vote—that the United Colonies are
free and independent states."

Rob was stunned. He knew there had been talk of independence among the radicals. But even George Washington
had been lukewarm toward such an idea when the fighting began. The rebels only wanted to force Great Britain to agree
that the colonies had the sole right to tax themselves.

"What does it mean?" he asked.

Aunt Lucy said, "It means that yesterday when you came
into Williamsburg, you were a British subject. Today you
owe absolute allegiance only to the independent Commonwealth of Virginia."

Something in her voice set prickles inside Rob's nose.

"Oh, there'll be more resolutions and voting," she said, "but
the thing is done. The British flag will never wave again from
the cupola of the Capitol there."

"Not even if *we* win the war?" Rob cried.

"We?" his aunt said. 'Rob, don't you understand? I'm a
patriot—and after today, *we rebels have to win.*"

8

Celebration

Everyone in Williamsburg seemed to be on the way to Waller's Grove to celebrate Virginia's resolution for independence. Men and women dressed in silk rode in carriages. Frontiersmen from beyond the Blue Ridge, in long hunting shirts, walked and carried their squirrel guns. Children skipped to keep up with fathers and mothers. Dogs frisked in and out among the people, barking to add to the excitement.

Rob heard drums beating as he hurried down Duke of Gloucester Street with the crowd. He didn't want to miss anything. His father would want to hear all about the celebration, too.

He stood on the sidewalk and watched experienced wilderness fighters pass with tomahawks swinging at their hips. Then militiamen paraded past him, muskets over their shoulders.

When the militia soldiers reached the grove, they formed squads and drilled smartly. Officers shouted commands.

Hundreds of pairs of feet came down to the thump of drums, left, right, left, right. The soldiers performed every order while the drums rolled.

Rob's heart began to thump to the stirring music. He forgot that these men were rebels and his enemies. They were Virginians and he was proud of them. Among the troops, he recognized and waved to a neighbor from Princess Anne.

The soldiers came to attention. The crowd turned toward a speaker who raised his hand for silence.

Rob couldn't see anything but the hand of the speaker over the heads of the tall men in front of him, but he heard the solemn voice.

"For days our thoughts have been employed on the great question—whether independence ought or ought not to be declared. The Commonwealth of Virginia has made a final decision."

The speaker paused. The expectant people remained quiet. Rob felt a lost feeling like homesickness rise up in him. He had grown up believing in England's fair treatment and justice toward all men. He was as proud of his English blood as he was of being a Virginian. He didn't know what to think now.

The speaker went on, "Virginia has declared herself an independent sovereignty, entitled to receive the absolute allegiance of all her citizens."

A roar rose from the crowd. Men tossed their hats into the air. Rob saw that every man, woman, and child here thought this bold defiance was the right thing to do.

He tried to squeeze under the arm of a tall militiaman so that he could see. The young man grinned and pulled Rob in front of him. He spoke with the drawl of a frontiersman.

"You mustn't miss this," he said. "Someday you can tell your grandchildren that you were here at the birth of a new nation—and we'll make her the best nation in the world as soon as we've chased the British back over the sea."

Rob looked up and thanked him. The militiaman smiled and there was a kind of glory in his eyes as if he saw something wonderful ahead which Rob could not see.

The people grew quiet. The speaker began to read the resolutions. The militiaman brought a piece of rock candy from his pocket and gave it to Rob. The candy melted on Rob's tongue while he listened.

After the reading of the resolutions, people cheered and hugged each other. Men shook hands. Soldiers shot muskets. Cannon boomed.

"Hurrah for Independence!" a man shouted. "Victory to America."

Someone cried, "The flag."

Rob turned with the crowd to see the new national banner rising above the Capitol building. The breeze caught it. The new flag rippled where the British flag used to fly.

For a long moment no one made a sound. Rob saw that women were crying. Grown men brushed their eyes with the backs of their hands. Rob felt his own throat grow tight.

Then drumsticks came down on drumheads in a burst of music. Soldiers saluted. People cheered again. Before he realized what he was doing, Rob shouted with them.

He stopped suddenly and was still. He hadn't meant to shout with the rebels. He hadn't really thought. The drums had stirred him to join in the rejoicing.

After the celebration, Rob walked home with sober thoughts. What would his father think if he knew that Rob had cheered for Virginia's independence? That he had taken a piece of candy from a friendly rebel militiaman? Would his father understand how Rob had been carried away by the excitement and contagious spirit of the people in Williamsburg today?

Rob was so absorbed in his remorse that he went past Aunt Lucy's home and came to the Blair house. He saw Mr. John Blair walking in his garden. Mr. Blair was dressed as if he, too, had just come from the celebration.

Rob knew that Mr. Blair was one of the most respected men in the town. He had served in the House of Burgesses.

He was also Aunt Lucy's neighbor. Rob had often helped himself to apples which fell over the fence into the street from the Blair yard. He wasn't afraid to go and speak to him.

"Mr. Blair," he asked, "what will happen now to loyalists?"

Mr. Blair seemed startled. Then he looked closer at Rob and smiled. "You're the boy who's visiting Miss Lucy, aren't you?"

"Yes, sir," Rob said.

"Well," Mr. Blair explained. "Loyalists will be asked to take an oath of allegiance to the new Commonwealth of Virginia. If they take it, I think most of them will be forgiven."

Rob thanked him and went home feeling better. He was sure his father would be interested to hear what Mr. Blair had said.

Early the next morning Rob took paper and pen to the gaol. He was pleased to find his father dressed in the clean linens he had brought. He had washed and shaved. Even the odors in the cells were not quite as bad as they had been yesterday.

"The gaoler must have wanted to celebrate, too," Captain

Roberts said. "He had the hall floors scrubbed with vinegar and threw fresh mint on the hay where we sleep."

"Then you knew about the celebration?" Rob asked.

"We couldn't see anything," his father answered, "but even the dead must have heard all the noise."

A man lying on the hay muttered, then began to cough. Rob knew he must be a loyalist like his father.

"Papa," Rob said, "I went—and afterwards I talked to Mr. Blair. He says loyalists can take an oath and be forgiven."

"You know I wouldn't take an oath not to fight against the rebels again," Captain Roberts said. "I only hope the Convention will hear my appeal and lighten my sentence. And not every rebel is as generous as John Blair." He handed Rob a newspaper. "Look at this," he said.

Rob held the folded page nearer the small window. He read from a speech made by a member of the Convention which was now governing Virginia. "A rattlesnake cannot turn into a butterfly. And an oath of allegiance will not turn a loyalist into a son-of-liberty!"

Rob gave the newspaper to his father without a word. He was distressed and tried to think of something to encourage his father.

"Aunt Lucy is a patriot," he said, "and she says some of the most honorable men in the Tidewater are for independence. How can men like Mr. Mason and Mr. Jefferson be so wrong?"

Captain Roberts turned quickly and gripped Rob's shoulder. "Can you understand what independence really means?" he demanded.

Rob was startled at the strain in his father's voice. Independence must be much worse than he had realized.

"Independence means," Captain Roberts said, "that revolution and rebellion have become patriotism. Loyalty has become treason."

Rob was shaken. Treason was turning against one's country. A man could be put to death for treason.

"Papa," he said, "no one can call you a traitor. You remained loyal to England and England's *our* country."

The man lying on the hay began to cough again. He rolled over and stared at Rob from bloodshot eyes. "England *was* our country," he said. "But not any more. Not after those rebels got through voting in the Convention.

"Rebels—calling *us* traitors! They're the ones who rebelled. Rebels started the war. They tried to get everyone to fight against the King by calling him a foreign tyrant who wanted to ruin America. England wouldn't ruin America any more than a mother would ruin her child."

He shook a bony finger at Rob. "Rebels said the King took away our freedom. Well, the King never took any freedom from me—or from your father here. The rebels took our freedom and left us to rot in this filthy gaol."

The man began to cough again and fell forward on the straw. Rob lifted the man's head while Captain Roberts brought water in a dipper and helped him to drink.

Then his father went to the door with Rob.

"He's sick," Rob said. "Why don't the rebels take him from the gaol as they did the old man yesterday?"

"Rebels won't let any of us go if we are strong and young enough to fight again—especially anyone who speaks out the way Tom Gordon does," Captain Roberts said. "But he's right. Independence is a terrible blow to loyalists, not only those in Virginia, but all of us throughout the colonies.

"Up to now we were fighting with and for our government, which was English no matter how American we thought ourselves to be. Now the new government is rebel. And the rebels are out to destroy anyone who doesn't think as they do."

Rob stood at the door. "Papa, they won't do anything to you, will they?" he asked.

His father looked at Rob, then changed the subject. "You'd better go now, Rob," he said. "I want to write a letter for you to take to your mother. The McClains are meeting you at the river this noon, aren't they?"

Rob nodded. "Aunt Lucy is lending me a horse and sending a servant to the river with me to bring it back."

"I'll have the letter written in a couple of hours," his father said. "Come for it before you leave for home."

Rob had planned to visit the shops to buy gifts to take to his mother and the girls. He found the shops closed this morning. Many of the townspeople were gathered at Bruton Parish Church for a day of fasting, thanksgiving, and prayers for independence. Rob had to content himself with looking in the shop windows.

He saw fancy curled wigs displayed at the wigmaker's. Beautiful leather-bound, gold-trimmed books at the book-binder's. In the windows of the apothecary were jars of all sizes, jars of rock candy, of dried herbs, and jars of strange substances whose names Rob couldn't even guess.

Finally he returned to the gaol for his father's letter. Captain Roberts had no sealing wax. He folded several pages of writing, tucked them inside Rob's shirt and anchored them under the waist band of his breeches.

"Don't touch the letter until you reach home," he said. "I don't want you to lose it. I've written many things which your mother must know."

"I'll come back to see you soon," Rob promised as he left.

At noon Rob reached the James River and found the *Oyster-Shell* waiting at the shore where it had left him three days ago. Captain McClain and Davy wanted to hear all about Captain Roberts and what was happening in Williamsburg. By the time Rob finished telling them about the dismal gaol, the parade and celebration, what everyone had said and done, the *Oyster-Shell* was long underway.

At Portsmouth Rob saw Lord Dunmore's fleet anchored in the harbor. Big and little ships of all kinds clung together like a floating town. Schooners, sloops, barques, and brigantines. The many masts and furled sails looked like a forest of dead trees creaking and groaning in the breeze. Rob turned away from the sad, far-off cries of the people crowded on the decks.

On the shore were artillerymen and British soldiers in bright red coats. Rob was puzzled by the swarm of townspeople coming and going along the roads.

Captain McClain drew the *Oyster-Shell* closer to the docks. He called to be recognized and allowed to pass up the Elizabeth River. Rob watched men, women, and children crowded on the wharves. Furniture and bedding were stacked high. Old people and sick people were hauled on carts. Frightened children were crying.

"What's the matter?" Rob asked. "Where are all these people going?"

"They're loyalists trying to leave while they can," Davy answered. "Now that the Convention declared for independence, they're afraid. Loyalists are fleeing to England, to Canada and Bermuda, wherever they think they'll be safe."

"You mean," Rob said, "they're so afraid, they'll leave their homes to live in a strange land—even before the rebels *make* them go?"

"Aye, lad," Captain McClain said. "These are dark and bewildered days for Britons who wouldn't turn against their King."

He was busy at the helm until the *Oyster-Shell* was safely into the channel. Then he asked, "Lad, what *was* Captain Robert's sentence? Dinna he say?"

Rob realized that his father had never actually stated what his sentence was.

"I told you," Rob said. "He was sentenced by the County Commissioner's Court of Accomack to the Williamsburg gaol as a prisoner of war. But Papa said not to fret, he had appealed to the Convention. He's probably written all about it in the letter I'm taking to Mama."

9

Two Letters

Captain McClain sailed the *Oyster-Shell* cautiously up the creek channel to her anchorage. "'Tis late, lad," he said. "You can't find your way through the swamp and woods in the dark. Stay the night with us."

By the light from candles in pierced tin lanterns hung in the hold, Rob helped Davy set a cold supper on the table. He grinned as they began to eat and said, "No mugs of milk this time. Are there no more cows to be foraged from the woods?"

Davy smiled but spoke seriously, "Foraging and provisioning the ships is more dangerous since Lee's militiamen have built another post at Norfolk. They scout Portsmouth constantly. We never know when his shirtmen may be hiding in the woods along the shore to attack us."

The ship rocked and creaked. Rob glanced quickly over his shoulder.

"Aye, lad," Captain McClain said. "Major-General Lee

posted a letter to warn the inhabitants of Portsmouth and Princess Anne county to mend their ways. Show it to Rob, Davy."

Davy opened a sea chest and brought forth a printed hand-bill. Rob took it and read the open letter:

As we have undoubted intelligence that Dunmore's Fleet and Army are amply and constantly supplied with provisions and refreshments of every kind from that tract of country lying between the Southern and Eastern Branches, as well as from Tanner's Creek, and that the positive ordinance levelled by the Convention against this form of treason was totally disregarded; I do order the removal of all persons caught in such treason, removal without exception, for even the women and children have learned the art and practiced the office of spies.

Rob drew a deep breath. "You can't help any more then?" he said.

Davy looked at his grandfather. The old man's mouth was grim.

"We dinna say we *mended* our ways," he said. "We're only more careful."

"Will you dare cross the bay again to load horses?" Rob asked.

"Aye, the need is great, and the rebels have not won the war—by declaring independence," Captain McClain said. "But we'll heed the danger and wait a time now."

"Please, when you do go, take me?" Rob asked.

Captain McClain frowned.

Rob pleaded, "If we win the war, Papa will surely be safe. Loading the horses is one way I can help Papa."

"When you put it that way," Captain McClain said.

Davy smiled. "He means you can go," he said. "I'll come for you when it's safer."

At midmorning Rob came from the woods and crossed the field toward the stable. He heard Becky shout. "Here he is. Rob's home."

His family was on the porch to greet him. His mother said, "Did you see your father? Is he well?"

Rob hesitated. He didn't want to tell her about the dirt and darkness and smells of the gaol. "He isn't sick," he said finally. "He's in Williamsburg gaol. He wrote you a letter."

Rob brought the crumpled folded papers from inside his shirt. His mother took them. Everyone followed her into the dining room.

"Read it aloud, Mama," Anne said.

"Sh-h-h," Mrs. Roberts said. "If you want to hear, be quiet and listen."

She read to them.

> With pleasure, my dear, I learned from Rob that you are well except for Sally's feverish cold. Kiss the little duck for me. And if she is not yet well, I have a new remedy from the ships' doctor which I use very successfully for my men with stomach disorders, ague, and fevers of all kinds.
>
> Send Juba for Vitriolated Tartar. Use 20 grains of it with 20 grains of Ixlap. It is the best purge of any for all bilious complaints. Use a teaspoon of sugar or rum to take off the disagreeable taste. For Sally, ten grains each should be enough— for Juba or any of you, the full dose.

How I wish I were able to be with my darlings, but as you know by now, I am a prisoner of war in Williamsburg gaol. You have heard how I was taken by surprise on Accomack when my ship went aground in a storm.

I cannot tell you how sad it was to see, among the rebels who captured me, men who had been my friends for years. They ordered me on shore without clothing, except that I wore, and treated me very airily.

I was taken before a County Court of Commissioners on Accomack. In this country where I formerly lived in the greatest harmony with all rank, male and female, young and old, they were greatly altered. Few would speak to me. None would show mercy.

My dear wife, I felt it better to write you the bad news which follows. I did not tell Rob and burden him with the sad knowledge until he was home and you could comfort one another.

The court directed my entire estate to be sold and I am to be imprisoned for the duration of the war. This is the most severe sentence to be passed upon a loyalist to this date.

The court had read to me a defense of its verdict as follows:

It is common justice that, if virtuous citizens in defence of their natural rights, risk their lives, liberty, and property on their success; vicious citizens, who side with tyranny and oppression, should at least hazard their property.

I know you are shocked, my dear wife, that in this unnatural war, I am branded a vicious citizen, traitor, and jailed for treason, for remaining loyal to our King and England.

Yet have hope! I have appealed to the Convention to hear and reconsider my case. I reminded them that I am an officer and a gentleman, entitled to the well-known justice of the English. Surely some of the delegates' hearts will be touched. There is hardly a man among them who does not have one relative who is a loyalist. One of the Randolph brothers is with us. Even the famous Benjamin Franklin has a Tory son. God grant that the members of the Convention will remember our common English heritage.

I am to be removed from Williamsburg gaol and sent to a prison somewhere in the north. I was told that my knowledge of the Virginia countryside made it too dangerous to keep me here. If I managed to escape, I would be able again to help Governor Dunmore provision his ships.

By the time you read this, I will be on board a ship on my way to exile in a northern prison. I know not where I am going. I will write as soon as I am allowed.

Your affectionate and loving husband,
CHARLES

Mrs. Roberts stopped reading and held the letter with both hands against her dress. She was trembling.

Rob hadn't moved, neither had the girls. Even Sally was quiet although she couldn't understand enough to know that her father was gone, no one knew where. They couldn't even visit him now. And their home was to be sold as a state forfeit. No wonder his father had appealed to the Convention to lighten such a severe sentence.

Rob's heart was beating fast, but he still could not feel afraid. It didn't seem true. This house, the whole plantation had belonged to the Roberts family for more than a hundred years. No one would take it from them. Surely the Convention would reverse the County Court's sentence.

"Mama," he said. "Wherever Papa is going, maybe it's no worse than the gaol. And as soon as the war's over, he'll come home. Maybe soon—if the British send troops to help Lord Dunmore and we all help."

His mother seemed not to hear him. She excused herself and went to her bedchamber. Anne ran into the garden. Sally sat on the floor and played with her kitten.

"Rob," Becky asked. "Did Uncle Charles say where Papa is?"

Rob shook his head, troubled. If Captain Roberts had good news about his brother, John, he surely would have sent it to

Becky. "Uncle John wasn't among the prisoners at the gaol, anyway," he said.

"It's six months since Papa brought me here," Becky said. "I haven't had a word."

"It isn't easy to find a way to send a letter," Rob comforted her. "He may be fighting somewhere."

"He could be sick," Becky said in a small voice, "or —."

Rob interrupted her hastily. "I'll ask Davy if he can learn where Uncle John is," he said. "Davy promised to come for me the next time they go to load horses."

10

Island Horses

R ob stood on the garden porch and watched for Juba to return on his old mule with the weekly newspaper. During the six weeks since Rob's return from Williamsburg, no word had come from his father. And no word from Becky's father. He hadn't heard from Davy. The *Virginia Gazette* was his only source of information.

Late in May, Rob had read of a battle between the rebel forces on shore and Dunmore's ships in the harbor. The cannon fire from shore had been so heavy that Dunmore's fleet had been forced to sail away and leave Portsmouth to the rebels. Rob wondered if the *Oyster-Shell* had been captured in this skirmish? Were Davy and his grandfather safe or prisoners like his father?

A later *Gazette* described Dunmore's landing on Gwynn's Island off Gloucester. Here the Governor entrenched on the western shore where he waited for help from the British. But the Virginia navy had overtaken and captured, in Chesapeake Bay, the transport of British troops sent to aid Dunmore.

By the first of July a large number of militiamen had gathered on the mainland opposite Gwynn's Island. The rebel troops were commanded by Andrew Lewis, an officer who had learned to fight in the Indian Wars. Only the lack of boats kept the rebel militiamen from attacking the British and loyalist forces on the island. The newspaper stated that the resourceful General Lewis would soon find a way to get at Dunmore.

Rob frowned. Even the loyalists had lost respect for Lord Dunmore who never seemed to do the right thing at the right time. But if he were defeated and driven from the bay, what would become of the loyal Americans who had joined him and fought for their King? Loyalists would be alone and unprotected in their own country. Could they expect mercy from rebel neighbors, angered by losses in battle?

No one had come to force the sale of his home, Rob thought, perhaps because Portsmouth was now in the hands of the rebels and Dunmore could no longer receive provisions by way of the river. Or perhaps the authorities were waiting for his father's appeal to be heard before the Convention. Every day that his family was allowed to remain on the plantation, brought greater hope to Rob. Maybe their home would be saved and his father would be exchanged for a rebel prisoner of war.

He heard someone whistling and turned. It was not Juba on the mule. A tall boy with a shock of red hair was crossing the garden.

"Davy," Rob cried and ran to meet him. "I was afraid you were a prisoner."

"No," Davy said, "we've been very careful. We've fished every day as usual. We brought our catch in to the dock and sold it to townspeople and rebel soldiers alike. Grandpa thinks the rebels trust us now and we can risk a trip across the bay."

"To load horses?" Rob asked.

"Aye," Davy said. "We need all the help we can get. Will your mother let you go? We'll be gone three days."

"She wants to help win the war and bring Papa home as much as I do," Rob said, "I'll go tell her."

Davy and Rob stood on deck while Captain McClain steered the *Oyster-Shell* across the bay. "We like to reach the pens by dusk," Davy said. "The moon tonight will be just right, light enough to load the horses—but not so bright that our ships can be seen at a distance."

Captain McClain sailed his ship into an inlet on Accomack across the channel from Gwynn's Island.

"This is our rendezvous with the horse transports," Davy explained. "Men have brought the horses to the shore to meet us. It's the safest place—the Virginia Navy isn't likely to be in these waters near Dunmore's fleet."

Rob caught sight of three large ships moving slowly as close to shore as they could come. In the dusk, he could scarcely make out the misty gray hulls cutting through the dark blue chop of the water. But their cabin lanterns were lit, yellow pinpoints of light to warn other ships to keep their distance.

"We're here, lads, and the tide will soon be low," Captain McClain said. "Splash ashore."

Rob followed the Captain and Davy into the dory which their big Negro had lowered for them. All four began to row.

They waded ashore and frightened some gulls who rose

with cries into the night. They stumbled through sand, past the broken hull of a shipwrecked vessel, through salt marsh that sucked at their ankles, and reached a little rise.

"This rise is a natural pen," Davy said. "A bit of firm earth surrounded by sinking swamp which the horses are afraid to enter."

Rob heard a snort and saw a pair of eyeballs in the dark before he made out the shadowy shape of a horse.

The horse had heard the boys. It reared and trumpeted a warning. All at once the rise was covered with the dark shapes of horses, racing, wheeling, squealing. Their eyes were like giant fireflies passing in the darkness.

Rob's heart raced. He felt he couldn't move even if the horses ran right over him. They came at him, almost upon him, then broke and whirled. He felt the flick of a long tail as it whipped his face. He heard heavy breathing and frightened

neighing. Then he saw several small colts trailing their mothers and he was moved.

"The poor little things," he said.

"We don't take the mares with colts," Davy said, "but sometimes they mix in when the men drive the horses here."

From all sides of the rise, men shouted. They turned the horses who circled. It was time to begin the drive to the shore.

Rob and Davy took places in two lines of men who formed human fences. Between the two lines was left a wide lane which led to the dories on the beach. Rob and Davy yelled and flung wide their arms whenever a wild horse tried to leap over the men and escape.

There were more men at the dories. Ropes were put on the horses' necks. Men in rowboats led and guided them to swim to the transport ships. Here men waited with slings of sailcloth to place under the belly of each horse. Ropes on block

and tackle lifted the horse from the water to the deck where he was secured in the hold below.

"There's sweet hay in the hold to soothe them," Davy told Rob, "though I doubt they give it much heed tonight."

Half the night passed before all the horses were loaded into the ships. Rob was hoarse from shouting and so tired that he could scarcely pull himself over the side of the dory when the work was done.

They had rowed part way back to the *Oyster-Shell*, in deep water, when Rob heard a splashing under the rim of the dory. He thought it might be a big fish flopping in fright at the oars, until he heard the whinny of a little colt lost from its mother.

He leaned over the dory rail. There, almost under his hand, was a small head with golden eyes reflecting the moonlight. The colt was struggling to keep its nostrils above water.

"Hold the oars," Rob called, resting his own. He leaned over the rail and caught the colt's mane and pulled it near enough to get his arms under the belly. The golden eyed colt was no larger than a shepherd dog.

"Steady me, Davy," Rob called.

Davy held Rob's legs while he lifted the colt into the dory. The toy colt was shivering from the cold water. Rob took off his jacket and wrapped it around the colt's body.

It wasn't afraid but pressed against Rob's knees and nuzzled his hand as if it expected to be fed.

"Can I keep him?" Rob asked.

"We can't risk taking him back," Captain McClain said, "and he surely can't swim to shore. He's yours."

When they reached the *Oyster-Shell*, Rob carried the colt

to the cabin. He and Davy mixed a paste of ground maize and water. The colt licked it from Rob's palm and gulped. It was plain to see that he wanted milk.

"You'll have milk as soon as we get home," Rob promised.

He rubbed the colt dry. Its hide was a light golden color. The colt nudged his face and whinnied. Rob remembered Midnight who had always recognized his step before he reached the stable and nickered to him. He longed to see his black filly again.

Captain McClain had the *Oyster-Shell* under sail.

"Isn't he going to rest?" Rob asked, falling onto a bunk.

"The ships never stay together any longer than they have to," Davy said. "We don't want to attract attention. Grandpa and I take turns at the tiller."

Davy lay on the bunk opposite Rob. The colt stood in the narrow passage between the boys. Rob fell asleep with his arm over the colt's neck.

Sometime later, Davy shook Rob's shoulder. "Come on deck," he said. "The sky looks like it's on fire over Gwynn's Island way."

Rob scrambled up the ladder after Davy.

A red glow lay far away on the water. Suddenly it flamed high. The glow leaped across the water to flare in a new place, leaped and flared again, a relay of racing rosy light.

"It's like a forest fire leaping from treetop to treetop," Rob cried, "but trees don't grow on water."

"They must be shipmasts on fire," Davy said.

"Aye, lad," Captain McClain said. "Must be the rebel attack on Dunmore. From the looks of it, half his fleet's afire."

It was an eerie sight to see the dots of flame burst new

against a black sky, yet hear no battle sound from the rebel cannon which must be bombarding the ships.

Finally the Captain said, "Ah-h-h, there's no help we can give them."

He was an old man and weary with the work of the night, yet Rob thought that he seemed to age many more years as he watched the fires spread on the water. He went below.

Davy took the tiller. Rob decided to stay with him.

"I wish I knew what was happening—who was winning?" Rob said.

"Aye," Davy agreed soberly. "We're either *better* off or *worse* off—when this fight is done."

Rob watched the way ahead. The sea was so quiet in the starlit gloom, that the *Oyster-Shell* might have been a ghost ship skimming over the dark water. The breeze was steady.

There wasn't a quiver in the bulging sail overhead, and no creaking of the mast.

Suddenly Rob thought he saw the shadowy outline of a great schooner bearing down on them, ready to pass to starboard side. He caught Davy's wrist and squeezed hard.

"There," he whispered, "abreast of us now. See her?"

Davy nodded. "Maybe she won't see us."

"She's crowding us," Rob said. "She's trying to capture us."

"Get Grandpa," Davy said. He swung the tiller hard over to turn the ship away, although he must have known that he could not outrun the schooner.

Rob went down the ladder and woke Captain McClain, expecting every moment to hear the boom of a gun overhead and a voice bellow for their surrender.

When the old man and Rob reached deck, the schooner had moved on with all sails set. There wasn't a light on board and she was soon lost in the night.

Davy drew a long breath. "She could have rammed us. I never saw her until she was on us."

"Aye, she did not mean you to," Captain McClain said thoughtfully. "She was running from something or someone. Let me take the tiller, lad. She may not be the only ship running this night."

He was right. In a short time the schooner was followed by a ghostly parade of ships, sloops, barques, and brigantines, and more schooners with guns girdling their dark hulls.

Captain McClain kept the *Oyster-Shell* to the right of the ships' lane. At dawn the fleet was still passing. The last ships were slower. Rob could see their crippled masts and torn sails scorched by shells and fire. All flew the British flag.

"Dunmore's floating town," Captain McClain said. "The whole of it. I'm fearing he intends to leave for good this time."

No one spoke again. What was there to say? If Dunmore was really leaving Chesapeake Bay, the rebels would have their way in Tidewater Virginia. What chance, then, had families like his, Rob thought, who had declared for England? How would the victorious rebels treat his father if he was allowed exchange from prison? Rob went below and petted the golden colt, as much to comfort himself as it.

Captain McClain waited until he had reached anchorage and Rob was ready to leave for home. Then he gave Rob a letter.

"Last night a man on Accomack gave me this letter," he said. "He asked me to take it to the family of Captain Charles Roberts."

Rob took the folded papers and his hand trembled. The letter must be from his father, the first word since late May and this was the tenth of July.

"Better read it, lad," the Captain said gently. "I've word-of-mouth message to go with it."

Rob broke the red wax seal and saw his father's handwriting. Tears of relief prickled in his nose. He read:

Providence, Rhode Island

My dear family, I have been imprisoned here with no way to send you word until now. I send this letter by a sincere friend and good man, Walter Kerr, who is returning to Accomack under a flag in order to take his family to safety in England. Although sympathetic to our cause, he never took up arms against the rebels. They are happy enough to let him go in peace and leave his estates to them!

I would spare you what I must now say; my appeal was turned down by the Convention. Our home and all we have is forfeit to the state. We own nothing in this world but our lives.

Mr. Kerr has agreed to make arrangements to hire a ship large enough to take you to England with his family. I have sent a letter to my cousin, Lady Jane Brown, in London. You will find welcome in her home. There I will join you as soon as the British are able to have me exchanged for a rebel officer who is our prisoner, for I can never return to Virginia.

My dear wife, I know how sad you will be to leave the home you love so much. I have no other choice, for any man that ever had any connection with Lord Dunmore most certainly will not be permitted to live any more in Virginia. As anxious as I am to remain all my days in this, my country, my affection for you will not let me think of it any longer. Many an uneasy hour I have spent wondering if our home is already taken—where you all are.

And I must heap more grief upon you. I learned through other prisoners brought here that my brother John died of smallpox on one of Lord Dunmore's warships. Tell Becky that her father was buried at sea with clergy, that she is our daughter from this time on. She is to go to England with you and we will always look after her.

Rob could not read any more. He looked at Captain McClain and Davy, and saw the sympathy in their faces.

"Did the man on Accomack, last night, tell you that we must leave our home to live in England?" Rob asked.

"No," the Captain said, "but I guessed it. The messenger

said to tell your mother that Mr. Kerr has chartered a ship to sail from Norfolk harbor a week Tuesday. Mr. Kerr will send a carriage for you the day before."

Rob swallowed. Such a short time. The colt nuzzled his hand and he petted it. What would he do with the golden colt now? He wished he could carry it home and give it to Becky when she heard about her father's death. But the colt was too small to stand the long stormy voyage to England with them.

"Davy," he said, "you can have the colt."

"I'll keep him—until you come back," Davy said.

Rob shook his head. There was nothing to come back to, with his home gone and few friends left in Virginia. He didn't try to say goodbye, but walked away into the woods.

11

Rob's Choice

A week never went faster, Rob thought. Boxes and packages were piled in the hall near the door to the garden. He knew all the packages could not go in the carriage tomorrow. Yet these treasures were few compared to those which must be left behind.

Mrs. Roberts hurried across the upstairs hall with a beautiful yellow dress over her arm. It was the dress she had worn on the night of Anne's party eight months ago, the night the rebels captured Dunmore's post at Great Bridge, the night Philip Moore left to join the militia and changed from friend to enemy.

Rob never dreamed, then, that the rebels would capture and burn Norfolk, drive Dunmore's fleet from the harbor at Portsmouth and, finally, from all of Chesapeake Bay. He could scarcely believe it now. He had to keep reminding himself that it was done; his father a prisoner, his home to be sold, and he must live in an alien land.

"Rob," his mother called from the top of the stairs, "please help Becky with her packages."

Rob began to climb the steps. He could hear his mother comforting her old nurse, Mima, who wept because she was too old to go on the long voyage.

Mrs. Roberts had been worried about what was to become of the three faithful servants who had never known any home but hers. She had decided to take Juba to England and send Mima and Lulu to Williamsburg.

"Cousin Lucy always envied me your cooking," she told Lulu, "and she loves you, Mima. You brought up both of us."

Rob had been surprised at his mother's strength after she read his father's letter. He knew how much she hated to leave her home. She dreaded the long sea voyage and openly worried about where she would go on a ship in a thunderstorm. But she managed to do the thousand and one things which had to be done to get ready to leave.

Becky met Rob at the head of the stairs and gave him two of her largest bundles.

"Be careful of this one, Rob," she said. "I wrapped one of Mama's teacups in the middle of all my petticoats, so it won't break. The cup is the only thing I took from home when Papa brought me here."

Becky, too, had been brave, Rob thought. She had cried for her father but began at once to help Anne and Mrs. Roberts pack.

They placed her packages with the others in the hall.

"I hope Philip Moore gets here before we have to leave," Becky said.

Rob frowned. Juba had brought Anne a letter from Philip Moore. The young man wrote that he had heard of the Convention's denial of Captain Roberts' appeal. He intended to ask for leave and come to see if he could be of any help. Rob didn't want anything from a rebel, no matter how good a friend and companion he once had been.

"I hope Mama won't let him in the house if he comes," Rob said.

Becky looked at him in astonishment. "If a gentleman wants to help her, why shouldn't she allow him to?" Becky asked.

Rob knew this was his mother's logic, too, but it wasn't his.

"Aunt Margaret has to have someone take Mima and Lulu to Williamsburg," Becky added. "She says Philip Moore is a reliable young man and she can trust them to him."

Rob didn't want to owe a rebel anything, even kindness. He went outdoors and sat on the steps of the porch. Becky followed and sat beside him.

"I don't like rebels either," she said, "but if they win the war, we'll have to live with them—when we come back."

"Come back?" Rob cried. "Didn't you read Papa's letter? We have no home—no horses—nothing. We *can't* come back!"

"Remember what Mr. Moore taught us when we were in school," Becky said. "Most people who came to America didn't have much to begin with. They worked the land and lived in cabins."

"We never did," Rob said. "And when the rebels are living

in my beautiful home, I'll not return to be called traitor. Or live like a pioneer among them—poor!"

"I will, if it's the only way I can come back to Virginia," Becky said.

Rob stared out over the fields and pastures where he and his father used to ride. The sight of the woods brought back the memory of Midnight and the night the raiders stole her. He stood up and walked fast down the garden path so Becky could not see him cry.

Then he saw a man riding a horse past the stable, through the orchard, directly toward the garden. It was a black horse.

Rob stopped. He couldn't breathe for a moment. Then he whistled the way he used to call Midnight at the paddock gate.

The black horse pricked up her ears and nickered. She trotted faster. She reached Rob and nuzzled his hair. He put an arm over her head and pressed his forehead against her glossy neck.

"Midnight," he said.

He saw that the man on her back was Philip Moore. Rob wanted to shove him off his horse and pummel him, but it wouldn't do any good.

"How could you come here again?" he cried, "on my horse —that you rebels stole."

"Listen, Rob," Philip Moore said. "I bought Midnight because I knew she belonged to you."

"Bought?" Rob said.

Philip Moore dismounted. "I saw a soldier riding her," he said, "the night we drove Dunmore from Gwynn's Island."

"Then you were in the battle, the night the ships sailed away like ghosts in the dark," Rob said. He saw that Philip Moore didn't know what he was talking about.

The young man went on, "Later I found the soldier who owned Midnight. I asked him to trade horses with me. He refused. I gave him my horse, my watch, and a month's pay, all I had. That's how I bought Midnight for you, Rob."

Rob blinked. He didn't know what to say. How could he allow himself to be grateful to a rebel?

"You know I have to leave for England—and Midnight can't go," he said.

"I'll do my best to keep her," Philip Moore answered, "until you come home."

This is what Davy had said when Rob had given him the golden colt. Becky had said, "Until we come back." Everyone acted as if he had a home to return to when they knew he didn't.

"Why don't you take Midnight to the stable and feed her," Philip Moore said, "while I find Anne."

Rob had forgotten what it felt like to be astride Midnight. She tossed her head and began to trot when she felt the touch of his knees on her sides. Something seemed to turn over inside Rob. He had to close his eyes for a moment.

Midnight remembered where to go. She started off toward the fields and pastures as if she knew he wanted to ride his own horse once more over his own land.

The sun warmed his back. The breeze cooled his face. He felt alive for the first time since he had read his father's letter and learned that he had to leave his home and country.

The odor of damp turf, kicked up by Midnight's hoofs, came to him, of apples ripening in the orchard, of pines in the woods. These were scents and sights he wanted to forget if he must live an exile in an alien land. Yet he knew he could never forget them.

He remembered that Midnight should be fed, and tried to turn her toward the stable. She pulled at the reins and began to run for the pure joy of running. Rob's heart beat faster as he felt the power of her muscles under his knees. He wanted to shout as he had that day in Williamsburg when the people cheered for the new flag rising above the Capitol.

Rob thought of the tall militiaman who had given him a rock candy. There had been a glory in the man's eyes which shook Rob. He had seemed to see something wonderful in the future which Rob could not see.

He had said, "You can tell your grandchildren that you were here—at the birth of a new nation—and we'll make her the greatest nation in the world."

"We." The rebel had said *we*.

Suddenly Rob knew that no matter who won the war, this was still his country. His father and he had not fought against America, but for her. In a revolution, both sides were fighting for the same country, only they couldn't agree on what was best for her. Captain McClain, Davy, all loyalists believed that the argument with England should be settled without bloodshed or independence.

His father's belief had brought heartache, defeat, and the loss of his home. But it didn't make him or Rob a traitor.

Rob would go to England. He would go to school and

learn all the things a gentleman must learn. But he would not remain an exile forever. He was an American and he wouldn't forget that. Virginia was his home.

He stretched along Midnight's neck and let her go.

"You remember me," he said, "until I come back."

Chronology

HISTORICAL EVENTS mentioned in this book:

June 8, 1775

Lord Dunmore, British appointed governor of Virginia, fled Williamsburg. With his family and followers, Dunmore lived on a British warship in Norfolk Harbor and controlled the surrounding area.

November 25, 1775

Colonel William Woodford with the Second Virginia Regiment arrived from Williamsburg, to threaten Dunmore at Norfolk.

December 9, 1775

Woodford's rebels defeated the British regulars and loyalists at the Battle of Great Bridge. Shortly after, the rebels entered the town of Norfolk where skirmishes, fires, and looting demolished two-thirds of Norfolk by January 1, 1776.

February 6, 1776   The rebel commander ordered the remainder of the town of Norfolk burned to deprive Dunmore of a place to come ashore. Dunmore, then, moved his fleet of ships and head-quarters to the town and harbor of Portsmouth.

March 29, 1776   Major-General Charles Lee arrived in Williamsburg to take charge of all colonial troops, and planned to at-tack Dunmore at Portsmouth.

May 6, 1776   The Virginia House of Burgesses, oldest representative body of govern-ment in British America, made the last entry in its Journal.

May 15, 1776   The new Convention in Williams-burg declared that Virginia was an independent commonwealth and re-solved to ask the Continental Con-gress to declare that *all* the American colonies were free of British rule.

May 16, 1776   A Celebration of Independence in Williamsburg.

May 17, 1776   Day of prayer, thanksgiving, and fasting in Bruton Parish Church.

May 20, 1776   Rebels attacked Dunmore at Ports-mouth. A few days later Dunmore sailed away and stationed his troops on Gwynn's Island off the coast of Gloucester.

July 9, 1776

General Lewis and the rebel militia attacked Gwynn's Island. Without waiting to take from the island either sick men or supplies, Dunmore sailed his entire fleet across Chesapeake Bay at night, and finally returned to England.